THE DOCTOR OF PIMLICO

Being the Disclosure of a Great Crime

WILLIAM LE QUEUX

First published by Cassell, 1919

LONDON BOUND
Oleander Press
16 Orchard Street
Cambridge
CB1 1JT

This edition © Oleander Press 2013

ISBN: 9781909349735
Printed in England
Cover design: Ayshea Carter (manganese@ntlworld.com)

CONTENTS

THE DOCTOR OF PIMLICO

CHAPTER I

IN WHICH CERTAIN SUSPICIONS ARE EXCITED

A grey, sunless morning on the Firth of Tay.

Across a wide, sandy waste stretching away to the misty sea at Budden, four men were walking. Two wore uniform – one an alert, grey-haired general, sharp and brusque in manner, with many war ribbons across his tunic; the other a tall, thin-faced staff captain, who wore the tartan of the Gordon Highlanders. With them were two civilians, both in rough shooting-jackets and breeches, one about forty-five, the other a few years his junior.

"Can you see them, Fellowes?" asked the general of the long-legged captain, scanning the distant horizon with those sharp grey eyes which had carried him safely through many campaigns.

"No, sir," replied the captain, who was carrying the other's mackintosh. "I fancy they must be farther over to the left, behind those low mounds yonder."

"Haven't brought their battery into position yet, I suppose," snapped the old officer, as he swung along with the two civilians beside him.

Fred Tredennick, the taller of the two civilians, walked with a gait decidedly military, for, indeed, he was a retired major, and as the general had made a tour of inspection of the camp prior to walking towards where the mountain battery was manœuvring, he had been chatting with him upon technical matters.

"I thought you'd like to see this mountain battery, Fetherston,"

1

exclaimed the general, addressing the other civilian. "We have lots of them on the Indian frontier, of course, and there were many of ours in Italy and Serbia."

"I'm delighted to come with you on this tour of inspection, General. As you know, I'm keenly interested in military affairs – and especially in the reorganisation of the Army after the war," replied Walter Fetherston, a dark, well-set-up man of forty, with a round, merry face and a pair of eyes which, behind their gold pince-nez, showed a good-humoured twinkle.

Of the four men, General Sir Hugh Elcombe and Walter Fetherston were, perhaps, equally distinguished. The former, as all the world knows, had had a brilliant career in Afghanistan, in Egypt, Burma, Tirah, the Transvaal, and in France, and now held an appointment as inspector of artillery.

The latter was a man of entirely different stamp. As he spoke he gesticulated slightly, and no second glance was needed to realise that he was a thorough-going cosmopolitan.

By many years of life on the Continent he had acquired a half-foreign appearance. Indeed, a keen observer would probably have noticed that his clothes had been cut by a foreign tailor, and that his boots, long, narrow and rather square-toed, bore the stamp of the Italian boot-maker. When he made any humorous remark he had the habit of slightly closing the left eye in order to emphasise it, while he usually walked with his left hand behind his back, and was hardly ever seen without a cigarette. Those cigarettes were one of his idiosyncrasies. They were delicious, of a brand unobtainable by the public, and made from tobacco grown in one of the Balkan States. With them he had, both before the war and after, been constantly supplied by a certain European sovereign whose personal friend he was. They bore the royal crown and cipher, but even to his most intimate acquaintance Walter Fetherston had never betrayed the reason why he was the recipient of so many favours from the monarch in question.

Easy-going to a degree, full of open-hearted bonhomie, possessing an unruffled temper, and apparently without a single care in all the world, he seldom, if ever, spoke of himself. He never mentioned either his own doings or his friends'. He was essentially a mysterious man – a man of moods and of strong prejudices.

More than one person who had met him casually had hinted that his substantial income was derived from sources that would not bear investigation – that he was mixed up with certain financial adventurers. Others declared that he was possessed of a considerable fortune that had been left him by an uncle who had been a dealer in precious stones in Hatton Garden. The truth was, however, that Walter Fetherston was a writer of popular novels, and from their sale alone he derived a handsome income.

The mystery stories of Walter Fetherston were world-famous. Wherever the English language was spoken this shrewd-eyed, smiling man's books were read, while translations of them appeared as feuilletons in various languages in the principal Continental journals. One could scarcely take up an English newspaper without seeing mention of his name, for he was one of the most popular authors of the day.

It is a generally accepted axiom that a public man cannot afford to be modest in these go-ahead days of "boom." Yet Fetherston was one of the most retiring of men. English society had tried in vain to allure him – he courted no personal popularity. Beyond his quiet-spoken literary agent, who arranged his affairs and took financial responsibility from his shoulders, his publishers, and perhaps half a dozen intimate friends, he was scarcely recognised in his true character. Indeed, his whereabouts were seldom known save to his agent and his only brother, so elusive

3

was he and so careful to establish a second self.

He had never married. It was whispered that he had once had a serious affair of the heart abroad. But that was a matter of long ago.

Shoals of invitations arrived at his London clubs each season, but they usually reached him in some out-of-the-world corner of Europe, and he would read them with a smile and cast them to the winds.

He took the keenest delight in evading the world that pressed him. His curious hatred of his own popularity was to everyone a mystery. His intimate friends, of whom Fred Tredennick was one, had whispered that, in order to efface his identity, he was known in certain circles abroad by the name of Maltwood. This was quite true. In London he was a member of White's and the Devonshire as Fetherston. There was a reason why on the Continent and elsewhere he should pass as Mr. Maltwood, but his friends could never discover it, so carefully did he conceal it.

Walter Fetherston was a writer of breathless mystery – but he was the essence of mystery himself. Once the reader took up a book of his he never laid it down until he had read the final chapter. You, my reader, have more than once found yourself beneath his strange spell. And what was the secret of his success? He had been asked by numberless interviewers, and to them all he had made the same stereotyped reply: "I live the mysteries I write."

He seemed annoyed by his own success. Other writers suffered from that complaint known as "swelled head," but Walter Fetherston never. He lived mostly abroad in order to avoid the penalty which all the famous must pay, travelling constantly and known mostly by his assumed name of Maltwood.

And behind all this some mystery lay. He was essentially a man of secrets.

Some people declared that he had married ten years ago, and gave a circumstantial account of how he had wedded the daughter of a noble Spanish house, but that a month later she had been accidentally drowned in the Bay of Fontarabia, and that the tragedy had ever preyed upon his mind. But upon his feminine entanglements he was ever silent. He was a merry fellow, full of bright humour, and excellent company. But to the world he wore a mask that was impenetrable.

At that moment he was shooting with his old friend Tredennick, who lived close to St. Fillans, on the picturesque Loch Earn, when the general, hearing of his presence in the neighbourhood, had sent him an invitation to accompany him on his inspection.

Walter had accepted for one reason only. In the invitation the general had remarked that he and his stepdaughter Enid were staying at the Panmure Hotel at Monifieth - so well known to golfers - and that after the inspection he hoped they would lunch together.

Now, Walter had met Enid Orlebar six months before at Biarritz, where she had been nursing at the Croix Rouge Hospital in the Hôtel du Palais, and the memory of that meeting had lingered with him. He had long desired to see her again, for her pale beauty had somehow attracted him - attracted him in a manner that no woman's face had ever attracted him before.

Hitherto he had held cynical notions concerning love and matrimony, but ever since he had met Enid Orlebar in that winter hotel beside the sea, and had afterwards discovered her to be stepdaughter of Sir Hugh Elcombe, he had found himself reflecting upon his own loneliness.

At luncheon he was to come face to face with her again. It was of this he was thinking more than of the merits of mountain batteries or the difficulties of limbering or unlimbering.

"See! There they are!" exclaimed the general, suddenly pointing with his gloved hand.

Fetherston strained his eyes towards the horizon, but declared that he could detect nothing.

"They're lying behind that rising ground to the left of the magazine yonder," declared the general, whose keen vision had so often served him in good stead. Then, turning on his heel and scanning the grey horizon seaward, he added: "They're going to fire out on to the Gaa between those two lighthouses on Buddon Ness. By Jove!" he laughed, "the men in them will get a bit of a shock."

"I shouldn't care much to be there, sir," remarked Tredennick.

"No," laughed the general. "But really there's no danger – except that we're just in the line of their fire."

So they struck off to the left and approached the position by a circuitous route, being greeted by the colonel and other officers, to whom the visit of Sir Hugh Elcombe had been a considerable surprise.

The serviceable-looking guns were already mounted and in position, the range had been found; the reserves, the ponies and the pipers were lying concealed in a depression close at hand when they arrived.

The general, after a swift glance around, stood with legs apart and arms folded to watch, while Fetherston and Tredennick, with field-glasses, had halted a little distance away.

A sharp word of command was given, when next instant the first gun boomed forth, and a shell went screaming through the air towards the low range of sand-hills in the distance.

The general grunted. He was a man of few words, but a typical British officer of the type which has made the Empire and won the war against the Huns. He glanced at the watch upon his wrist, adjusted his monocle, and said something in an undertone to the captain.

The firing proceeded, while Fetherston, his ears dulled by the constant roar, watched the bursting shells with interest.

"I wonder what the lighthouse men think of it now?" he laughed, turning to his friend. "A misdirected shot would send them quickly to kingdom come!"

Time after time the range was increased, until, at last, the shells were dropped just at the spot intended. As each left the gun it shrieked overhead, while the flash could be seen long before the report reached the ear.

"We'll see in a few moments how quickly they can get away," the general said, as he approached Fetherston.

Then the order was given to cease fire. Words of command sounded, and were repeated in the rear, where ponies and men lay hidden. The guns were run back under cover, and with lightning rapidity dismounted, taken to pieces, and loaded upon the backs of the ponies, together with the leather ammunition cases - which looked like men's suit cases - and other impedimenta.

The order was given to march, and, headed by the pipers, who commenced their inspiring skirl to the beat of the drums, they moved away over the rough, broken ground, the general standing astraddle and watching it all through his monocle with critical eye, and keeping up a fire of sarcastic comment directed at the colonel.

"Why!" he cried sharply in his low, strident voice, "what's that bay there? Too weak for the work - no good. You want better stuff than that. An axle yonder not packed properly! . . . And look at that black pony - came out of a governess-cart, I should think! . . . Hey, you man there, you don't want to hang on that pack! Men get lazy and want the pony to help them along. And you —" he cried, as a pony, heavily laden with part of a gun, came down an almost perpendicular incline. "Let that animal find his way down alone. Do you hear?"

Then, after much manœuvring, he caused them to take up another position, unlimber their guns, and fire.

When this had been accomplished he called the officers together and, his monocle in his eye, severely criticised their performance, declaring that they had exposed themselves so fully to the enemy that ere they had had time to fire they would have been shelled out of their position.

The spare ammunition was exposed all over the place, some of the reserves were not under cover, and the battery commander so exposed himself that he'd have been a dead man before the first shot. "You must do better than this – much better. That's all."

Then the four walked across to the Panmure Hotel at Monifieth.

Walter Fetherston held his breath. His lips were pressed tightly together, his brows contracted. He was again to meet Enid Orlebar.

He shot a covert glance at the general walking at his side. In his eyes showed an unusual expression, half of suspicion, half of curiosity.

Next instant, however, it had vanished, and he laughed loudly at a story Tredennick was telling.

CHAPTER II

THE COMING OF A STRANGER

Enid was standing on the steps of the hotel when the men arrived.

For a second Walter glanced into her splendid eyes, and then bowed over her hand in his foreign way, a murmured expression of pleasure escaping his lips.

About twenty-two, tall and slim, she presented a complete and typical picture of the outdoor girl, dressed as she was in a grey jumper trimmed with purple, a short golfing skirt, her tweed hat to match trimmed with the feathers of a cock pheasant.

Essentially a sportswoman, she could handle gun or rod, ride to hounds, or drive a motor-car with equal skill, and as stepdaughter of Sir Hugh she had had experience on the Indian frontier and in Egypt.

Her father had been British Minister at the Hague, and afterwards at Stockholm, but after his death her mother had married Sir Hugh, and had become Lady Elcombe. Nowadays, however, the latter was somewhat of an invalid, and seldom left their London house in Hill Street. Therefore, Enid was usually chaperoned by Mrs. Caldwell, wife of the well-known K.C., and with her she generally spent her winters on the Continent.

Blanche, Sir Hugh's daughter by his first wife, had married Paul Le Pontois, who had been a captain in the 114th Regiment of Artillery of the French Army during the war, and lived with her husband in France. She seldom came to England, though at frequent intervals her father

9

went over to visit her.

When Walter Fetherston took his seat beside Enid Orlebar at the luncheon table a flood of strange recollections crowded upon his mind – those walks along the Miramar, that excursion to Pampeluna, and those curious facts which she had unwittingly revealed to him in the course of their confidential chats. He remembered their leave-taking, and how, as he had sat in the *rapide* for Paris, he had made a solemn vow never again to set eyes upon her.

There was a reason why he should not – a strong but mysterious reason.

Yet he had come there of his own will to meet her again – drawn there irresistibly by some unseen influence which she possessed.

Was it her beauty that had attracted him? Yes – he was compelled to admit that it was. As a rule he avoided the society of women. To his intimates he had laid down the maxim: "Don't marry; keep a dog if you want a faithful companion." And yet he was once again at the side of this fair-faced woman.

None around the table were aware of their previous meeting, and all were too busy chattering to notice the covert glances which he shot at her. He was noting her great beauty, sitting there entranced by it – he, the man of double personality, who, under an assumed name, lived that gay life of the Continent, known in society in twenty different cities, and yet in England practically unknown in his real self.

Yes, Enid Orlebar was beautiful. Surely there could be few fairer women than she in this our land of fair women!

Turning upon him, she smiled gaily as she asked whether he had been interested in seeing a mountain battery at work.

Her fresh face, betraying, as it did, her love of a free, open-air life, was one of those strangely mysterious countenances met only once in a lifetime. It seemed to be the quintessence of pain and passion, conflict and agony, desire and despair. She was not one of those befrilled, fashion-plate dolls that one meets at the after-war crushes and dances, but was austerely simple in dress, with a face which betrayed a spiritual nobility, the very incarnation of modern womanhood, alive with modern self-knowledge, modern weariness and modern sadness.

Her beautiful hair, worn plain and smooth, was black as night – wonderful hair. But still more wonderful were those great, dark, velvety eyes, deep and unfathomable. In them the tragedy of life was tumultuously visible, yet they were serene, self-possessed, even steady in their quiet simplicity. To describe her features is not an easy task. They were clear-cut, with a purity of the lines of the nose and brow seldom seen in a woman's face, dark, well-arched eyebrows, a pretty mouth which had just escaped extreme sensuousness. Cheeks soft and delicately moulded, a chin pointed, a skin remarkable for its fineness and its clear pallor, the whole aspect of her face being that of sweetness combined with nobility and majesty. In it there was no dominant expression, for it seemed to be a mask waiting to be stirred into life.

Fetherston had known Sir Hugh slightly for several years, but as Enid had been so much abroad with Mrs. Caldwell, he had never met her until that accidental encounter in Biarritz.

"We've been up here six weeks," she was telling Fetherston. "Father always gets a lot of golf up here, you know, and I'm rather fond of it."

"I fear I'm too much of a foreigner nowadays to appreciate the game," Walter laughed. "Last season some Italians in Rome formed a club – the usual set of ultra-smart young counts and marquises – but when they found that it entailed the indignity of walking several miles they declared it to be a game only fit for the populace, and at once disbanded the association."

The men were discussing the work of the battery, for four of the officers had been invited, and the point raised was the range of mountain guns.

Walter Fetherston glanced at the general through his pince-nez with a curious expression, but he did not join in the conversation.

Enid's eyes met his, and the pair exchanged curiously significant glances.

He bent to pick up his serviette, and in doing so he whispered to her: "I must see you outside for a moment before I go. Go out, and I'll join you."

Therefore, when the meal had concluded, the girl went forth into the secluded garden at the rear of the hotel, where in a few moments the man joined her at a spot where they could not be overlooked.

She turned towards him, separate, remote, incongruous, her dark eyes showing an angry flash in them.

"Why have you come here?" she demanded with indignation. The whole aspect of her face was tragic.

"To see you again," was his brief reply. "Before we parted at Biarritz you lied to me," he added in a hard tone.

She held her breath, staring straight into his eyes.

"I - I don't understand you!" she stammered. "You are here to torment - to persecute me!"

"I asked you a question, Enid, but in response you told me a deliberate lie. Think - recall that circumstance, and tell me the truth," he said very quietly.

She was silent for a moment. Then, with her mouth drawn to hardness, she replied: "Yes, it is true - I lied to you, just as you have lied to me. Remember what you told me that moonlit night when we walked by the sea towards the Grotto of Love. I was a fool to have believed in you - to have trusted you as I did! You left me, and, though I wrote time after time to your club, you refused to send me a single line."

"Because - because, Enid, I dared not," replied her companion.

"Why not?" she demanded quickly. "You told me that you loved me, yet - yet your own actions have shown that you lied to me!"

"No," he protested in a low, earnest, hoarse voice; "I told you the truth, Enid, but —"

"But what?" she interrupted in quickly earnestness.

"Well," he replied after a brief pause, "the fact is that I am compelled to wear a mask, even to you, the woman I love. I cannot tell you the truth - I cannot, dearest, for your own sake."

"And you expect me to believe this lame story - eh?" she laughed. She was pale and fragile, yet she seemed to expand and to dilate with force and energy.

"Enid," he answered in a low voice, with honesty in his eyes, "I would rather sacrifice my great love for you than betray the trust I hold most sacred. So great is my love for you, rather would I never look upon your dear face again than reveal to you the tragic truth and bring upon you unhappiness and despair."

"Walter," she replied in a trembling voice, looking straight into his countenance with those wonderful dark eyes wherein her soul brimmed over with weary emotion and fatigued passion, "I repeat all that I told you on that calm night beside the sea. I love you; I think of you day by day, hour by hour. But you have lied to me, and therefore I hate myself for having so foolishly placed my trust in you."

He had resolved to preserve his great secret - a secret that none should know.

"Very well," he sighed, shrugging his shoulders. "These recriminations are really all useless. Ah, if you only knew the truth, Enid! If I only dared to reveal to you the hideous facts. But I refuse - they are too tragic, too terrible. Better that we should part now, and that you should remain in ignorance - better by far, for you. You believe that I am deceiving you. Well, I'm frank and admit that I am; but it is with a distinct purpose – for your own sake."

He held forth his hand, and slowly she took it. In silence he bowed over it, his lips compressed; then, turning upon his heel, he went down the gravelled walk back to the hotel, which, some ten minutes later, he left with Fred Tredennick, catching the train back to Dundee and on to Perth.

He was in no way a man to wear his heart upon his sleeve, therefore he chatted gaily with his friend and listened to Fred's extravagant admiration of Enid's beauty. He congratulated himself that his old friend was in ignorance of the truth.

A curious incident occurred at the hotel that same evening, however, which, had Walter been aware of it, would probably have caused him considerable uneasiness and alarm. Just before seven o'clock a tall, rather thin, middle-aged, narrow-eyed man, dressed in dark grey tweeds, entered the hall of the hotel and inquired for Henry, the head waiter. He was well dressed and bore an almost professional air.

The white-headed old man quickly appeared, when the stranger, whose moustache was carefully trimmed and who wore a ruby ring upon his white hand, made an anxious inquiry whether Fetherston, whom he minutely described, had been there that day. At first the head waiter hesitated and was uncommunicative, but, the stranger having uttered a few low words, Henry's manner instantly changed. He started, looked in wonder into the stranger's face, and, taking him into the smoking-room – at that moment unoccupied – he allowed himself to be closely questioned regarding the general and his stepdaughter, as well as the man who had that day been their guest. The stranger was a man of quick actions, and his inquiries were sharp and to the point.

"You say that Mr. Fetherston met the young lady outside after luncheon, and they had an argument in secret, eh?" asked the stranger.

Henry replied in the affirmative, declaring that he unfortunately could not overhear the subject under discussion. But he believed the pair had quarrelled.

"And where has Mr. Fetherston gone?" asked his keen-eyed questioner.

"He is, I believe, the guest of Major Tredennick, who lives on the other side of Perthshire at Invermay on Loch Earn."

"And the young lady goes back to Hill Street with her stepfather, eh?"

"On Wednesday."

"Good!" was the stranger's reply. Then, thanking the head waiter for the information in a sharp, businesslike voice, and handing him five shillings, he took the train back from Monifieth to Dundee, and went direct to the chief post-office.

From there he dispatched a carefully constructed cipher telegram to an address in the Boulevard Anspach, in Brussels, afterwards lighting an excellent cigar and strolling along the busy street with an air of supreme self-satisfaction.

"If this man, Fetherston, has discovered the truth, as I fear he has done," the hard-faced man muttered to himself, "then by his action today he has sealed his own doom! – and Enid Orlebar herself will silence him!"

CHAPTER III

INTRODUCES DOCTOR WEIRMARSH

Three days had elapsed.

In the dingy back room of a dull, drab house in the Vauxhall Bridge Road, close to Victoria Station in London, the narrow-eyed man who had so closely questioned old Henry at the Panmure Hotel, sat at an old mahogany writing-table reading a long letter written upon thin foreign notepaper.

The incandescent gas-lamp shed a cold glare across the room. On one side of the smoke-grimed apartment was a shabby leather couch, on the other side a long nest of drawers, while beside the fireplace was an expanding gas-bracket placed in such a position that it could be used to examine anyone seated in the big armchair. Pervading the dingy apartment was a faint smell of carbolic, for it was a consulting-room, and the man so intent upon the letter was Dr. Weirmarsh, the hard-working practitioner so well known among the lower classes in Pimlico.

Those who pass along the Vauxhall Bridge Road know well that house with its curtains yellow with smoke – the one which stands back behind a small strip of smoke-begrimed garden. Over the gate is a red lamp, and upon the railings a brass plate with the name: "Mr. Weirmarsh, Surgeon."

About three years previously he had bought the practice from old Dr. Bland, but he lived alone, a silent and unsociable man, with a deaf old housekeeper, although he had achieved a considerable reputation among his patients in the neighbouring by-streets. But his practice was not wholly confined to the poorer classes, for he was often consulted by well-dressed members of the foreign colony – on account, probably, of his linguistic attainments. A foreigner with an imperfect knowledge of English naturally prefers a doctor to whom he can speak in his own tongue. Therefore, as Weirmarsh spoke French, Italian and Spanish with equal fluency, it was not surprising that he had formed quite a large practice among foreign residents.

His appearance, however, was the reverse of prepossessing, and his movements were often most erratic. About his aquiline face was a shrewd and distrustful expression, while his keen, dark eyes, too narrowly set, were curiously shifty and searching. When absent, as he often was, a young fellow named Shipley acted as locum tenens, but so eccentric was he that even Shipley knew nothing of the engagements which took him from home so frequently.

George Weirmarsh was a man of few friends and fewer words. He lived for himself alone, devoting himself assiduously to his practice, and doing much painstaking writing at the table whereat he now sat, or else, when absent, travelling swiftly with aims that were ever mysterious.

He had had a dozen or so patients that evening, but the last had gone, and he had settled himself to read the letter which had arrived when his little waiting-room had been full of people.

As he read he made scribbled notes on a piece of paper upon his blotting-pad, his thin, white hand, delicate as a woman's, bearing that splendid ruby ring, his one possession in which he took a pride.

"Ah!" he remarked to himself in a hard tone of sarcasm, "what fools the shrewdest of men are sometimes over a woman! So at last he's fallen – like the others – and the secret will be mine. Most excellent! After all, every man has one weak point in his armour, and I was not mistaken."

Then he paused, and, leaning his chin upon his hand, looked straight before him, deep in reflection.

"I have few fears – very few," he remarked to himself, "but the greatest is of Walter Fetherston. What does he know? – that's the chief question. If he has discovered the truth – if he knows my real name and who I am – then the game's up, and my best course is to leave England. And yet there is another way," he went on, speaking slowly to himself – "to close his lips. Dead men tell no tales."

He sat for a long time, his narrow-set eyes staring into space, contemplating a crime. As a medical man, he knew a dozen ingenious ways by which Walter Fetherston might be sent to his grave in circumstances that would appear perfectly natural. His gaze at last wandered to the book-case opposite, and became centred upon a thick, brown-covered, dirty volume by a writer named Taylor. That book contained much that might be of interest to him in the near future.

All of a sudden the handle of the door turned, and Mrs. Kelsey, the old housekeeper, in rusty black, admitted Enid Orlebar without the ceremony of asking permission to enter.

The girl was dressed in a pearl grey and pink sports coat, with a large black hat, and carried a silver chain handbag. Around her throat was a white feather boa, while her features were half concealed by the veil she wore.

"Ah, my dear young lady," cried Weirmarsh, rising quickly and greeting her, while next moment he turned to his table and hastily concealed the foreign letter and notes, "I had quite forgotten that you were to consult me. Pray forgive me."

"There is nothing to forgive," the beautiful girl replied in a low, colourless voice, when the housekeeper had disappeared, and she had seated herself in the big leather armchair in which so many patients daily sat. "You ordered me to come here to you, and I have come."

"Against your will, eh?" he asked slowly, with a strange look in his keen eyes.

"I am perfectly well now. I do not see why my stepfather should betray such anxiety on my account."

"The general is greatly concerned about you," Weirmarsh said, seated cross-legged at his writing-chair, toying with his pen and looking into the girl's handsome face.

"He wished me to see you. That is why I wrote to you."

"Well," she said, wavering beneath his sharp glance, "I am here. What do you wish?"

"I wish to have a little private talk with you, Miss Enid," he replied thoughtfully, stroking his small greyish moustache, "a talk concerning your own welfare."

"But I am not ill," she cried. "I don't see why you should desire me to come to you tonight."

"I have my own reasons, my dear young lady," was the man's firm response, his eyes fixed immovably upon hers. "And I think you know me well enough to be aware that when Dr. Weirmarsh sets his mind upon a thing he is not easily turned aside."

A slight, almost imperceptible, shudder ran through her. But Weirmarsh detected it, and knew that this girl of extraordinary and mysterious charm was as wax in his hands. In the presence of the man who had cast such a strange spell about her she was utterly helpless. There was no suggestion of hypnotism – she herself scouted the idea – yet ever since Sir Hugh had taken her to consult this man of medicine at a small suburban villa, five years ago, he had entered her life never again to leave it.

She realised herself irresistibly in his power whenever she felt his presence near her. At his bidding she came and went, and against her better nature she acted as he commanded.

He had cured her of an attack of nerves five years ago, but she had ever since been beneath his hated thraldom. His very eyes fascinated her with their sinister expression, yet to her he could do no wrong.

A thousand times she had endeavoured to break free from that strong but unseen influence, but she always became weak and easily led as soon as she fell beneath the extraordinary power which the obscure doctor possessed. Time after time he called her to his side, as on this occasion, on pretence of prescribing for her, and yet with an ulterior motive. Enid Orlebar was a useful tool in the hands of this man who was so unscrupulous.

She sighed, passing her gloved hand wearily across her hot brow. Strange how curiously his presence always affected her!

She had read in books of the mysteries of hypnotic suggestion, but she was far too practical to believe in that. This was not hypnotism, she often declared within herself, but some remarkable and unknown power possessed by this man who, beneath the guise of the hard-working surgeon, was engaged in schemes of remarkable ingenuity and wondrous magnitude.

He held her in the palm of his hand. He held her for life – or for death.

To her stepfather she had, times without number, expressed fear and horror of the sharp-eyed doctor, but Sir Hugh had only laughed at her fears and dismissed them as ridiculous. Dr. Weirmarsh was the general's friend.

Enid knew that there was some close association between the pair, but of its nature she was in complete ignorance. Often the doctor came to Hill Street and sat for long periods with the general in that small, cosy room which was his den. That they were business interviews there was no doubt, but the nature of the business was ever a mystery.

"I see by your face that, though there is a great improvement in you,

you are, nevertheless, far from well," the man said, his eyes still fixed upon her pale countenance.

"Dr. Weirmarsh," she protested, "this constant declaration that I am ill is awful. I tell you I am quite as well as you are yourself."

"Ah! There, I'm afraid, you are mistaken, my dear young lady," he replied. "You may feel well, but you are not in quite such good health as you imagine. The general is greatly concerned about you, and for that reason I wished to see you tonight," he added with a smile as, bending towards her, he asked her to remove her glove.

He took her wrist, holding his stop-watch in his other hand. "Huh!" he grunted, "just as I expected. You're a trifle low - a little run down. You want a change."

"But we only returned from Scotland yesterday!" she cried.

"The North does not suit such an exotic plant as yourself," he said. "Go South - the Riviera, Spain, Italy, or Egypt."

"I go with Mrs. Caldwell at the end of November."

"No," he said decisively, "you must go now."

"Why?" she asked, opening her eyes in astonishment at his dictatorial manner.

"Because —" and he hesitated, still gazing upon her with those strangely sinister eyes of his. "Well, Miss Enid, because a complete change will be beneficial to you in more ways than one," he replied with an air of mystery.

"I don't understand you," she declared.

"Probably not," he laughed, with that cynical air which so irritated her. She hated herself for coming to that detestable house of grim silence; yet his word to her was a command which she felt impelled by some strange force to fulfil with child-like obedience. "But I assure you I am advising you for your own benefit, my dear young lady."

"In what way?"

"Shall I speak plainly?" asked the man in whose power she was. "Will you forgive me if I so far intrude myself upon your private affairs as to give you a few words of advice?"

"Thank you, Dr. Weirmarsh, but I cannot see that my private affairs are any concern of yours," she replied with some hauteur. How often had she endeavoured in vain to break those invisible shackles?

"I am a very sincere friend of your stepfather, and I hope a sincere friend of yours also," he said with perfect coolness. "It is because of this I presume to advise you - but, of course —" And he hesitated, without concluding his sentence. His eyes were again fixed upon her as though gauging accurately the extent of his influence upon her.

"And what do you advise, pray?" she asked, "It seems that you have called me to you tonight in order to intrude upon my private affairs," she added, with her eyes flashing resentment.

"Well - yes, Miss Enid," he answered, his manner changing slightly. "The fact is, I wish to warn you against what must inevitably bring disaster both upon yourself and your family."

"Disaster?" she echoed. "I don't follow you."

"Then let me speak a little more plainly," he replied, his strange, close-set eyes staring into hers until she quivered beneath his cold, hard gaze. "You have recently become acquainted with Walter Fetherston. You met him at Biarritz six months ago, and on Monday last he lunched with you up at Monifieth. After luncheon you met him in the garden of the hotel, and —"

"How do you know all this?" she gasped, startled, yet fascinated by his gaze.

"My dear young lady," he laughed, "it is my business to know certain things - that is one of them."

She held her breath for a moment.

"And pray how does that concern you? What interest have you in my acquaintances?"

"A very keen one," was the prompt reply. "That man is dangerous to you - and to your family. The reason why I have asked you here tonight is to tell you that you must never meet him again. If you value your life, and that of your mother and her husband, avoid him as you would some venomous reptile. He is your most deadly enemy."

The girl was silent for a moment. Her great, dark eyes were fixed upon the threadbare carpet. What he told her was disconcerting, yet, knowing instinctively, as she did, how passionately Walter loved her, she could not bring herself to believe that he was really her enemy.

"No, Dr. Weirmarsh," she replied, raising her eyes again to his, "you are quite mistaken. I know Walter Fetherston better than you. Your allegation is false. You have told me this because - because you have some motive in parting us."

"Yes," he said frankly, "I have - *a strong motive.*"

"You do not conceal it?"

"No," he answered. "Were I a younger man you might, perhaps, accuse me of scheming to wriggle myself into your good graces, Miss Enid. But I am getting old, and, moreover, I'm a confirmed bachelor, therefore you cannot, I think, accuse me of such ulterior motives. No, I only point out this peril for your family's sake - and your own."

"Is Mr. Fetherston such an evil genius, then?" she asked. "The world knows him as a writer of strictly moral, if exciting, books."

"The books are one thing - the man himself another. Some men reflect their own souls in their works, others write but canting hypocrisy. It is so with Walter Fetherston - the man who has a dual personality and whose private life will not bear the light of publicity."

"You wish to prejudice me against him, eh?" she said in a hard tone.

"I merely wish to advise you for your good, my dear young lady," he said. "It is not for me, your medical man, to presume to dictate to you,

I know. But the general is my dear friend, therefore I feel it my duty to reveal to you the bitter truth."

Thoughts of Walter Fetherston, the man in whose eyes had shone the light of true honesty when he spoke, arose within her. She was well aware of all the curious gossip concerning the popular writer, whose eccentricities were so frequently hinted at in the gossipy newspapers, but she was convinced that she knew the real Fetherston behind the mask he so constantly wore.

This man before her was deceiving her. He had some sinister motive in thus endeavouring to plant seeds of suspicion within her mind. It was plain that he was endeavouring in some way to secure his own ends. Those ends, however, were a complete and inexplicable mystery.

"I cannot see that my friendship for Mr. Fetherston can have any interest for you," she replied. "Let us talk of something else."

"But it has," he persisted. "You must never meet that man again – you hear! Never – otherwise you will discover to your cost that my serious warning has a foundation only too solid; that he is your bitterest enemy posing as your most affectionate friend."

"I don't believe you, Dr. Weirmarsh!" she cried resentfully, springing to her feet. "I'll never believe you!"

"My dear young lady," the man exclaimed, "you are really quite unnerved tonight. The general was quite right. I will mix you a draught like the one you had before – perfectly innocuous – something to soothe those unstrung nerves of yours." And beneath his breath, as his cruel eyes twinkled, he added: "Something to bring reason to those warped and excited senses – something to sow within you suspicion and hatred of Walter Fetherston."

Then aloud he added, as he sprang to his feet: "Excuse me for a moment while I go and dispense it. I'll be back in a few seconds."

He left the room when, quick as lightning, Enid stretched forth her hand to the drawer of the writing-table into which she had seen the doctor toss the foreign letter he had been reading when she entered.

She drew it out, and scanned eagerly a dozen or so of the closely-written lines in Spanish.

Then she replaced it with trembling fingers, and, closing the drawer, sat staring straight before her – dumbfounded, rigid.

What was the mystery?

By the knowledge she had obtained she became forearmed – even defiant. In the light of that astounding discovery, she now read the mysterious Dr. Weirmarsh as she would an open book. She held her breath, and an expression of hatred escaped her lips.

When, a moment later, he brought her a pale-yellow draught in a graduated glass, she took it from his hand, and, drawing herself up in defiance, flung its contents behind her into the fireplace. She believed that at last she had conquered that strangely evil influence which, emanating from this obscure practitioner, had fallen upon her.

But the man only shrugged his shoulders and, turning from her, laughed unconcernedly. He knew that he held her in bonds stronger than steel, that his will was hers – for good or for evil.

CHAPTER IV

REVEALS TEMPTATION

"I tell you it can't be done – the risk is far too great!" declared Sir Hugh Elcombe, standing with his back to the fireplace in his cosy little den in Hill Street at noon next day.

"It must be done," answered Dr. Weirmarsh, who sat in the deep green leather armchair, with the tips of his fingers placed together.

The general glanced suspiciously at the door to reassure himself that it was closed.

"You ask too much," he said. Then, in a decisive voice, while his fingers toyed nervously with his monocle, he added, "I have resolved to end it once and for all."

The doctor looked at him with a strange expression in those cold, keen eyes of his and smiled, "I fear, Sir Hugh, that if you attempt to carry out such a decision you will find insuperable difficulties," he said quietly.

"I desire no good advice from you, Weirmarsh," the old general snapped. "I fully realise my position. You have cornered me – cut off my retreat – so I have placed my back against the wall."

"Good! And how will such an attitude benefit you, pray?"

"Understand, I am in no mood to be taunted by you!" the old man cried, with an angry flash in his eyes. "You very cleverly enticed me into the net, and now you are closing it about me."

"My dear Sir Hugh," replied the doctor, "ours was a mere business

26

transaction, surely. Carry your thoughts back to six years ago. After your brilliant military career you returned from India and found yourself, as so many of your profession find themselves, in very straitened circumstances. You were bound to keep up appearances, and, in order to do so, got into the hands of Eli Moser, the moneylender. You married Lady Orlebar, and had entered London society when, of a sudden, the scoundrelly usurer began to put the screw upon you. At that moment you - luckily, I think, for yourself - met me, and - well, I was your salvation, for I pointed out to you an easy way by which to pay your creditors and rearrange your affairs upon a sound financial basis. Indeed, I did it for you. I saved you from the moneylender. Did I not?"

He spoke in a calm, even tone, without once removing his eyes from the man who stood upon the hearthrug with bent head and folded arms.

"I know, Weirmarsh. It's true that you saved me from bankruptcy - but think what penalty I have paid by accepting your terms," he answered in a low, broken voice. "The devil tempted me, and I fell into your damnable net."

"I hardly think it necessary for you to put it that way," replied the doctor without the least sign of annoyance. "I showed you how you could secure quite a comfortable income, and you readily enough adopted my suggestion."

"Readily!" echoed the fine-looking old soldier. "Ah! You don't know what my decision cost me - it has cost me my very life."

"Nonsense, man," laughed the doctor scornfully. "You got out of the hands of the Jews, and ever since that day you haven't had five minutes' worry over your finances. I promised you I would provide you with an ample income, and —"

"And you've done so, Weirmarsh," cried the old general; "an income far greater than I expected. Yet what do I deserve?"

"My dear General," said the doctor quite calmly, "you're not yourself today; suffering from a slight attack of remorse, eh? It's a bad complaint; I've had it, and I know. But it's like the measles - you're very nearly certain to contract it once in a lifetime."

"Have you no pity for me?" snarled Sir Hugh, glaring at the narrow-eyed man seated before him. "Don't you realise that by this last demand of yours you've driven me into a corner?"

Weirmarsh's brows contracted slightly, and he shot an evil glance at the man before him - the man who was his victim. "But you must do it. You still want money - and lots of it, don't you?" he said in a low, decisive voice.

"I refuse, I tell you!" cried Sir Hugh angrily.

"Hush! Someone may overhear," the doctor said. "Is Enid at home?"

"Yes."

"I saw her last night, as you wished. She is not well. Her nerves are still in an extremely weak state," Weirmarsh said, in order to change the topic of conversation. "I think you should send her abroad out of the way - to the South somewhere."

"So she told me. I shall try and get Mrs. Caldwell to take her to Sicily - if you consider the air would be beneficial."

"Excellent - Palermo or Taormina - send the girl there as soon as ever you can. She seems unstrung, and may get worse; a change will certainly do her good," replied the man whose craft and cunning were unequalled. "I know," he added reflectively, "that Enid dislikes me - why, I can never make out."

"Instinct, I suppose, Weirmarsh," was the old man's reply. "She suspects that you hold me in your power, as you undoubtedly do."

"Now that is really a most silly idea of yours, Sir Hugh. Do get rid of it. Such a thought pains me to a great degree," declared the crafty-eyed man. "For these past years I have provided you with a good income, enabling you to keep up your position in the world, instead of - well, perhaps shivering on the Embankment at night and partaking of the hospitality of the charitably disposed. Yet you upbraid me as though I had treated you shabbily!" He spoke with an irritating air of superiority, for he knew that this man who occupied such a high position, who was an intimate friend and confidant of the Minister of War, and universally respected throughout the country, was but a tool in his unscrupulous hands.

"You ask me too much," exclaimed the grey-moustached officer in a hard, low voice.

"The request does not emanate from me," was the doctor's reply; "I am but the mouthpiece."

"Yes, the mouthpiece - but the eyes and ears also, Weirmarsh," replied Sir Hugh. "You bought me, body and soul, for a wage of five thousand pounds a year —"

"The salary of one of His Majesty's Ministers," interrupted the doctor. "It has been paid to you with regularity, together with certain extras. When you have wished for a loan of five hundred or so, I have never refused it."

"I quite admit that; but you've always received a *quid pro quo*," the general snapped. "Look at the thousands upon thousands I put through for you!"

"The whole transaction has from the beginning been a matter of business; and, as far as I am concerned, I have fulfilled my part of the contract."

The man standing upon the hearthrug sighed. "I suppose," he said, "that I really have no right to complain. I clutched at the straw you held out to me, and saved myself at a cost greater than the world can ever know. I hate myself for it. If I had then known what I know now concerning you and your friends, I would rather have blown out my

29

brains than have listened to your accursed words of temptation. The whole plot is damnable!"

"My dear fellow, I am not Mephistopheles," laughed the narrow-eyed doctor.

"You are worse," declared the general boldly. "You bought me body and soul, but by Heaven!" he cried, "you have not bought my family, sir!"

Weirmarsh moved uneasily in his chair.

"And so you refuse to do this service which I requested of you, yesterday, eh?" he asked very slowly.

"I do."

A silence fell between the two men, broken only by the low ticking of the little Sheraton clock upon the mantelshelf.

"Have you fully reflected upon what this refusal of yours may cost you, General?" asked the doctor in a slow, hard voice, his eyes fixed upon the other's countenance.

"It will cost me just as much as you decide it shall," was the response of the unhappy man, who found himself enmeshed by the crafty practitioner.

"You speak as though I were the principal, whereas I am but the agent," Weirmarsh protested.

"Principal or agent, my decision, Doctor, is irrevocable – I refuse to serve your accursed ends further."

"Really," laughed the other, still entirely unruffled, "your attitude today is quite amusing. You've got an attack of liver, and you should allow me to prescribe for you."

The general made a quick gesture of impatience, but did not reply.

It was upon the tip of Weirmarsh's tongue to refer to Walter Fetherston, but next instant he had reflected. If Sir Hugh really intended to abandon himself to remorse and make a fool of himself, why should he stretch forth a hand to save him?

That ugly revelations – very ugly ones – might result was quite within the range of possibility, therefore Weirmarsh, whose craft and cunning were amazing, intended to cover his own retreat behind the back of the very man whom he had denounced to Enid Orlebar.

He sat in silence, his finger-tips again joined, gazing upon the man who had swallowed that very alluring bait he had once placed before him.

He realised by Sir Hugh's manner that he regretted his recent action and was now overcome by remorse. Remorse meant exposure, and exposure meant prosecution – a great public prosecution, which, at all hazards, must not be allowed.

As he sat there he was actually calmly wondering whether this fine old officer with such a brilliant record would die in silence by his own hand and carry his secret to the grave, or whether he would leave behind some awkward written statement which would incriminate himself and those for whom he acted.

Suddenly Sir Hugh turned and, looking the doctor squarely in the face as though divining his inmost thoughts, said in a hoarse voice tremulous with emotion: "Ah, you need not trouble yourself further, Weirmarsh. I have a big dinner-party tonight, but by midnight I shall have paid the penalty which you have imposed upon me – I shall have ceased to live. I will die rather then serve you further!"

"Very well, my dear sir," replied the doctor, rising from his chair abruptly. "Of course, every man's life is his own property – you can take it if you think fit – but I assure you that such an event would not concern me in the least. I have already taken the precaution to appear with clean hands – should occasion require."

CHAPTER V

IN WHICH ENID ORLEBAR IS PUZZLED

That night, around the general's dinner-table in Hill Street, a dozen or so well-known men and women were assembled.

Sir Hugh Elcombe's dinners were always smart gatherings. The table was set with Georgian silver and decorated daintily with flowers, while several of the women wore splendid jewels. At the head sat Lady Elcombe, a quiet, rather fragile, calm-faced woman in black, whose countenance bore traces of long suffering, but whose smile was very sweet.

Among the guests was Walter Fetherston, whom the general had at last induced to visit him, and he had taken in Enid, who looked superb in a cream décolleté gown, and who wore round her throat a necklet of turquoise matrices, admirably suited to her half-barbaric beauty.

Fetherston had only accepted the general's invitation at her urgent desire, for she had written to White's telling him that it was imperative they should meet – she wished to consult him; she begged of him to forget the interview at Monifieth and return to her.

So, against his will, he had gone there, though the house and all it contained was hateful to him. With that terrible secret locked within his heart – that secret which gripped his very vitals and froze his blood – he looked upon the scene about him with horror and disgust. Indeed, it was only by dint of self-control that he could be civil to his host.

His fellow-guests were of divers types: a couple of peers and their womenkind, a popular actor-manager, two diplomats, and several military men of more or less note – two of them, like the host, occupying high positions at the War Office.

Such gatherings were of frequent occurrence at Hill Street. It was popularly supposed that Sir Hugh, by marrying His Majesty's Minister's widow, had married money, and was thus able to sustain the position he did. Other military men in his position found it difficult to make both ends meet, and many envied old Hugh Elcombe and his wealthy wife. They were unaware that Lady Orlebar, after the settlement of her husband's estate, had found herself with practically nothing, and that her marriage to Sir Hugh had been more to secure a home than anything else. Both had, alas, been equally deceived. The general, believing her to be rich, had been sadly disillusioned; while she, on her part, was equally filled with alarm when he revealed to her his penurious position.

The world, of course, knew nothing of this. Sir Hugh, ever since his re-marriage, had given good dinners and had been entertained in return, therefore everybody believed that he derived his unusually large income from his wife.

As he sat at table he laughed and chatted merrily with his guests, for on such occasions he was always good company. Different, indeed, was his attitude from when, at noon, he had stood with Weirmarsh in his own den and pronounced his own fate.

The man who held him in that strange thraldom was seated at the table. He had been invited three days ago, and had come there, perhaps, to taunt him with his presence in those the last few hours of his life.

Only once the two men exchanged glances, for Weirmarsh was devoting all his attention to young Lady Stockbridge. But when Sir Hugh encountered the doctor's gaze he saw in his eyes open defiance and triumph.

In ignorance of the keen interest which the doctor across the table felt in him, Walter Fetherston sat chatting and laughing with Enid. Once the doctor, to whom he had been introduced only half an hour before, addressed a remark to him to which he replied, at the same time reflecting within himself that Weirmarsh was quite a pleasant acquaintance.

He was unaware of that mysterious visit of inquiry to Monifieth, of that remarkable cipher telegram afterwards dispatched to Brussels, or even of the extraordinary influence that man in the well-worn evening suit possessed over both his host and the handsome girl beside him.

When the ladies had left the table the doctor set himself out over the cigarettes to become more friendly with the writer of fiction. Then afterwards he rose, and encountering his host, who had also risen and crossed the room, whispered in a voice of command: "You have reconsidered your decision! You will commit no foolish and cowardly act? I see it in your face. I shall call tomorrow at noon, and we will discuss the matter further."

The general did not reply for a few seconds. But Weirmarsh had already realised that reflection had brought his victim to a calmer state of mind.

"I will not listen to you," the old man growled.

"But I shall speak whether you listen or not. Remember, I am not a man to be fooled by talk. I shall be here at noon and lay before you a scheme perhaps a little more practicable than the last one." And with that he reached for some matches, turned upon his heel, and rejoined the man against whom he had warned Enid – the only man in the world whom he feared.

Before they rose Weirmarsh had ingratiated himself with his enemy. So clever was he that Fetherston, in ignorance as to whom his fellow-guest really was, save that he was a member of the medical profession, was actually congratulating himself that he had now met a man after his own heart.

At last they repaired to the pretty old-rose-and-gold drawing-room upstairs, an apartment in which great taste was displayed in decoration, and there several of the ladies sang or recited. One of them, a vivacious young Frenchwoman, was induced to give Barrois's romance, "J'ai vu fleurir notre dernier lilas!"

When she had concluded Enid, with whom Walter was seated, rose and passed into the small conservatory, which was prettily illuminated with fairy lights. As soon as they were alone she turned to him in eager distress, saying: "Walter, do, I beg of you, beware of that man!"

"Of what man?" he asked in quick surprise.

"Of Doctor Weirmarsh."

"Why? I don't know him. I never met him until tonight. Who is he?"

"My stepfather's friend, but my enemy - and yours," she cried quickly, placing her hand upon her heart as though to quell its throbbing.

"Is he well known?" inquired the novelist.

"No - only in Pimlico. He lives in Vauxhall Bridge Road, and his practice lies within a radius of half a mile of Victoria Station."

"And why is he my enemy?"

"Oh, that I cannot tell."

"Why is he your stepfather's friend?" asked Fetherston. "They certainly seem to be on very good terms."

"Doctor Weirmarsh's cunning and ingenuity are unequalled," she declared. "Over me, as over Sir Hugh, he has cast a kind of spell - a —"

Her companion laughed. "My dear Enid," he said, "spells are fictions of the past; nobody believes in them nowadays. He may possess some influence over you, but surely you are sufficiently strong-minded to resist his power, whatever it may be?"

"No," she replied, "I am not. For that reason I fear for myself – and for Sir Hugh. That man compelled Sir Hugh to take me to him for a consultation, and as soon as I was in his presence I knew that his will was mine – that I was powerless."

"I don't understand you," said Fetherston, much interested in this latest psychic problem.

"Neither do I understand myself," she answered in bewilderment. "To me this man's power, fascination – whatever you may term it – is a complete mystery."

"I will investigate it," said Fetherston promptly. "What is his address?"

She told him, and he scribbled it upon his shirt-cuff. Then, looking into her beautiful countenance, he asked: "Have you no idea of the nature of this man's influence over Sir Hugh?"

"None whatever. It is plain, however, that he is master over my stepfather's actions. My mother has often remarked to me upon it," was her response. "He comes here constantly, and remains for hours closeted with Sir Hugh in his study. So great is his influence that he orders our servants to do his bidding."

"And he compelled Sir Hugh to take you to his consulting room, eh? Under what pretext?"

"I was suffering from extreme nervousness, and he prescribed for me with beneficial effect," she said. "But ever since I have felt myself beneath his influence in a manner which I am utterly unable to describe. I do not believe in hypnotic suggestion, or it might be put down to that."

"But what is your theory?"

"I have none, except – well, except that this man, essentially a man of evil, possesses some occult influence which other men do not possess."

"Yours is not a weak nature, Enid," he declared. "You are not the sort of girl to fall beneath the influence of another."

"I think not," she laughed in reply. "And yet the truth is a hard and bitter one."

"Remain firm and determined to be mistress of your own actions," he urged, "and in the meantime I will cultivate the doctor's acquaintance and endeavour to investigate the cause of this remarkable influence of his."

Why did Doctor Weirmarsh possess such power over Sir Hugh? He wondered. Could it be that this man was actually in possession of the truth? Was he aware of that same terrible and hideous secret of which he himself was aware - a secret which, if exposed, would convulse the whole country, so shameful and scandalous was it!

He saw how pale and agitated Enid was. She had in her frantic anxiety sought his aid. Only a few days ago they had parted; yet now, in the moment of her fear and apprehension, she had recalled him to her side to seek his advice and protection.

She had not told him of that mysterious warning Weirmarsh had given her concerning him, or of his accurate knowledge of their acquaintanceship. She had purposely refrained from telling him this lest her words should unduly prejudice him. She had warned Walter that the doctor was his enemy - this, surely, was sufficient!

"Try and discover, if you can, the reason of the doctor's power over my father, and why he is for ever directing his actions," urged the girl. "For myself I care little; it is for Sir Hugh's sake that I am trying to break the bonds, if possible."

"You have no suspicion of the reason?" he repeated, looking seriously into her face. "You do not think that he holds some secret of your stepfather's? Undue influence can frequently be traced to such a source."

She shook her head in the negative, a blank look in her great, dark eyes.

"No," she replied, "it is all a mystery – one which I beg of you, Walter, to solve, and" – she faltered in a strange voice – "and to save me!"

He pressed her hand and gave her his promise. Then for a second she raised her full red lips to his, and together they passed

back into the drawing-room, where their re-entry in company did not escape the sharp eyes of the lonely doctor of Pimlico.

CHAPTER VI

BENEATH THE ELASTIC BAND

Walter Fetherston strolled back that night to the dingy chambers he rented in Holles Street, off Oxford Street, as a *pied-à-terre* when in London. He was full of apprehension, full of curiosity, as to who this Doctor Weirmarsh could be.

He entered his darkling, shabby old third-floor room and threw himself into the armchair before the fire to think. It was a room without beauty, merely walls, repapered once every twenty years, and furniture of the mid-Victorian era. The mantelshelf in the bedroom still bore stains from the medicine bottles which consoled the final hours of the last tenant, a man about whom a curious story was told.

It seems that he found a West End anchorage there, not when he had retired, but when he was in the very prime of life. He never told anyone that he was single; at the same time he never told anyone he was married. He just came and rented those three rooms, and there his man brought him his tea at ten o'clock every morning for thirty years. Then he dressed himself and went round to the Devonshire, in St. James's Street, and there remained till closing time, at two o'clock, every morning for thirty years. When his club closed in the dog-days for repairs he went to the club which received him. He never went out of town. He never slept a night away. He never had a visitor. He never received a letter, and, so far as his man was aware, never wrote one.

One morning he did not go through his usual programme. The

39

doctor was called, but during the next fortnight he died.

Within twelve hours, however, his widow and a family of grown-up children arrived, pleasant, cheerful, inquisitive people, who took away with them everything portable, greatly to the chagrin of the devoted old manservant who had been the tenant's single home-tie for thirty years.

It was these self-same, dull, monotonous chambers which Walter occupied. The old manservant was the self-same man who had so devotedly served the previous tenant. They suited Walter's purpose, for he was seldom in London, so old Hayden had the place to himself for many months every year. Of all the inhabitants of London chambers those are the most lonely who never wander away from London. But Walter was ever wandering, therefore he never noticed the shabbiness of the carpet, the dinginess of the furniture, or the dispiriting gloom of everything.

Like the previous tenant, Walter had no visitors and was mostly out all day. At evening he would write at the dusty old bureau in which the late tenant had kept locked his family treasures, or sit in the deep, old horsehair-covered chair with his feet upon the fender, as he did that night after returning from Hill Street.

The only innovation in those grimy rooms was a good-sized fireproof safe which stood in the corner hidden by a side-table, and from this Walter had taken a bundle of papers and carried them with him to his chair.

One by one he carefully went through them, until at last he found the document of which he was in search.

"Yes," he exclaimed to himself after he had scanned it, "so I was not mistaken after all! The mystery is deeper than I thought. By Jove! That fellow, Joseph Blot, alias Weirmarsh, alias Detmold, Ponting and half a dozen other names, no doubt, is playing a deep game – a dangerous customer evidently!"

Then, again returning to the safe, he took out a large packet of miscellaneous photographs of various persons secured by an elastic band. These he went rapidly through until he held one in his hand, an unmounted *carte-de-visite*, which he examined closely beneath the green-shaded reading-lamp.

It was a portrait of Doctor Weirmarsh, evidently taken a few years before, as he then wore a short pointed beard, whereas he was now shaven except for a moustache.

"No mistake about those features," he remarked to himself with evident satisfaction as, turning the photographic print, he took note of certain cabalistic numbers written in the corner, scribbling them in pencil upon his blotting-pad.

"I thought I recollected those curious eyes and that unusual breadth of forehead," he went on, speaking to himself, and again examining the pictured face through his gold pince-nez. "It's a long time since I looked at this photograph - fully five years. What would the amiable doctor think if he knew that I held the key which will unlock his past?"

He laughed lightly to himself, and, selecting a cigarette from the silver box, lit it.

Then he sat back in his big armchair, his eyes fixed upon the fire, contemplating what he realised to be a most exciting and complicated problem.

"This means that I must soon be upon the move again," he murmured to himself. "Enid has sought my assistance - she has asked me to save her, and I will exert my utmost endeavour to do so. But I see it will be difficult, very difficult. She is, no doubt, utterly unaware of the real identity of this brisk, hard-working doctor. And perhaps, after all," he added slowly, "it is best so - best that she remain in ignorance of this hideous, ghastly truth!"

At that same moment, while Walter Fetherston was preoccupied by these curious apprehensions, the original of that old *carte-de-visite* was seated in the lounge of the Savoy Hotel, smoking a cigar with a tall, broad-shouldered, red-bearded man who was evidently a foreigner.

He had left Hill Street five minutes after Fetherston, and driven down to the Savoy, where he had a rendezvous for supper with his friend. That he was an habitué there was patent from the fact that upon entering the restaurant, Alphonse, the *maître d'hôtel*, with his plan of the tables pinned upon the board, greeted him with, "Ah! Good evening, Docteur. Table vingt-six, Docteur Weirmarsh."

The scene was the same as it is every evening at the Savoy; the music, the smart dresses of the women, the flowers, the shaded lights, the chatter and the irresponsible laughter of the London world amusing itself after the stress of war.

You know it – why, therefore, should I describe it? Providing you possess an evening suit or a low-necked dress, you can always rub shoulders with the *monde* and the *demi-monde* of London at a cost of a few shillings a head.

The two men had supped and were chatting in French over their coffee and "triplesec." Gustav, Weirmarsh called his friend, and from his remarks it was apparent that he was a stranger to London. He was dressed with elegance. Upon the corner of his white lawn handkerchief a count's coronet was embroidered, and upon his cigar-case also was a coronet and a cipher. In his dress-shirt he wore a fine diamond, while upon the little finger of his left hand glittered a similar stone of great lustre.

The lights were half extinguished, and a porter's voice cried, "Time's up, ladies and gentlemen!" Those who were not habitués rose and commenced to file out, but the men and women who came to the restaurant each night sat undisturbed till the lights went up again and another ten minutes elapsed before the final request to leave was made.

The pair, seated away in a corner, had been chatting in an undertone when they were compelled to rise. Thereupon the doctor insisted that his friend, whose name was Gustav Heureux, should accompany him home. So twenty minutes later they alighted from a taxi-cab in the Vauxhall Bridge Road, and entered the shabby little room wherein Weirmarsh schemed and plotted.

The doctor produced from a cupboard some cognac and soda and a couple of glasses, and when they had lit cigars they sat down to resume their chat.

Alone there, the doctor spoke in English.

"You see," he explained, "it is a matter of the greatest importance – if we make this coup we can easily make a hundred thousand pounds within a fortnight. The general at first refused and became a trifle – well, just a trifle resentful, even vindictive; but by showing a bold front I've brought him round. Tomorrow I shall clinch the matter. That is my intention."

"It will be a brilliant snap, if you can actually accomplish it," was the red-bearded man's enthusiastic reply. He now spoke in English, but with a strong American accent. "I made an attempt two years ago, but failed, and narrowly escaped imprisonment."

"A dozen attempts have already been made, but all in vain," replied the doctor, drawing hard at his cigar. "Therefore, I'm all the more keen to secure success."

"You certainly have been very successful over here, Doctor," observed the foreigner, whose English had been acquired in America. "We have heard of you in New York, where you are upheld to us as a model. Jensen once told me that your methods were so ingenious as to be unassailable."

"Merely because I am well supplied with funds," answered the other with modesty. "Here, in England, as elsewhere, any man or woman can be bought – if you pay their price. There is only one section of the wonderful British public who cannot be purchased – the men and women who are in love with each other. Whenever I come up against Cupid, experience has taught me to retire deferentially, and wait until the love-fever has abated. It often turns to jealousy or hatred, and then the victims fall as easily as off a log. A jealous woman will betray any secret, even though it may hurry her lover to his grave. To me, my dear Gustav, this fevered world of London is all very amusing."

"And your profession as doctor must serve as a most excellent mask. Who would suspect you – a lonely bachelor in such quarters as these?" exclaimed his visitor.

"No one does suspect me," laughed the doctor with assurance. "Safety lies in pursuing my increasing practice, and devoting all my spare time to – well, to my real profession." He flicked the ash off his cigar as he spoke.

"Your friend, Elcombe, will have to be very careful. The peril is considerable in that quarter."

"I know that full well. But if he failed it would be he who would suffer – not I. As usual, I do not appear in the affair at all."

"That is just where you are so intensely clever and ingenious," declared Heureux. "In New York they speak of you as a perfect marvel of foresight and clever evasion."

"It is simply a matter of exercising one's wits," Weirmarsh laughed lightly. "I always complete my plans with great care before embarking upon them, and I make provision for every *contretemps* possible. It is the only way, if one desires success."

"And you have had success," remarked his companion. "Marked success in everything you have attempted. In New York we have not been nearly so fortunate. Those three articles in the *New York Sun* put the public on their guard, so that we dare not attempt any really bold move for fear of detection."

"You have worked a little too openly, I think," was Weirmarsh's reply. "But now that you have been sent to assist me, you will probably see that my methods differ somewhat from those of John Willoughby. Remember, he has just the same amount of money placed at his disposal as I have."

"And he is not nearly so successful," Heureux replied. "Perhaps it is because Americans are not so easily befooled as the English."

"And yet America is, *par excellence*, the country of bluff, of quackery in patent medicines, and of the booming of unworthy persons," the doctor laughed.

"It is fortunate, Doctor, that the public are in ignorance of the real nature of our work, isn't it, eh? Otherwise, you and I might experience rather rough handling if this house were mobbed."

Weirmarsh smiled grimly. "My dear Gustav," he laughed, "the British public, though of late they've browsed upon the hysterics of the popular Press, are already asleep again. It is not for us to arouse them. We profit by their heavy slumber, and this will be a rude awakening - a shock, depend upon it."

"We were speaking of Sir Hugh Elcombe," remarked the other. "He has been of use to us, eh?"

"Of considerable use, but his usefulness is all but ended," replied the doctor. "He will go to France before long, if he does not act as I direct."

"Into a veritable hornet's nest!" exclaimed the red-bearded man. He recognised a strange expression upon the doctor's face, and added, "Ah, I see. This move is intentional, eh? He has served our purpose, and you now deem it wise that - er - disaster should befall him across the Channel, eh?"

The doctor smiled in the affirmative.

"And the girl you spoke of, Enid Orlebar?"

"The girl will share the same fate as her stepfather," was Weirmarsh's hard response. "We cannot risk betrayal."

"Then she knows something?"

"She may or she may not. In any case, however, she constitutes a danger, a grave danger, that must, at all costs, be removed." And looking into the other's face, he added, "You understand me?"

"Perfectly."

Just before two o'clock Gustav Heureux left the frowsy house in Vauxhall Bridge Road and walked through the silent street into Victoria Street.

He was unaware, however, that on the opposite side of the road an ill-dressed man had for a full hour been lurking in a doorway, or that when he came down the doctor's steps, the mysterious midnight watcher strolled noiselessly after him.

CHAPTER VII

CONCERNING THE VELVET HAND

On the rising ground half-way between Wimborne and Poole, in Dorsetshire, up a narrow by-road which leads to the beautiful woods, lies the tiny hamlet of Idsworth, a secluded little place of about forty inhabitants, extremely rural and extremely picturesque.

Standing alone half-way up the hill, and surrounded by trees, was an old-world thatched cottage, half-timbered, with high, red-brick chimneys, quaint gables and tiny dormer windows – a delightful old Elizabethan house with a comfortable, homely look. Behind it a well-kept flower garden, with a tree-fringed meadow beyond, while the well-rolled gravelled walks, the rustic fencing, and the pretty curtains at the casements betrayed the fact that the rustic homestead was not the residence of a villager.

As a matter of fact it belonged to a Mr. John Maltwood, a bachelor, whom Idsworth believed to be in business in London, and who came there at intervals for fresh air and rest. His visits were not very frequent. Sometimes he would be absent for many months, and at others he would remain there for weeks at a time, with a cheery word always for the labourers on their way home from work, and always with his hand in his pocket in the cause of charity.

John Maltwood, the quiet, youngish-looking man in the gold pince-nez, was popular everywhere over the countryside. He did not court the society of the local parsons and their wives, nor did he return

47

any of the calls made upon him. His excuse was that he was at Idsworth for rest, and not for social duties. This very independence of his endeared him to the villagers, who always spoke of him as "one of the right sort."

At noon on the day following the dinner at Hill Street, Walter Fetherston – known at Idsworth as Mr. Maltwood – alighted from the station fly, and was met at the cottage gate by the smiling, pleasant-faced woman in a clean apron who acted as caretaker.

He divested himself of his overcoat in the tiny entrance-hall, passed into a small room, with the great open hearth, where in days long ago the bacon was smoked, and along a passage into the long, old-world dining-room, with its low ceiling with great dark beams, its solemn-ticking, brass-faced grandfather clock, and its profusion of old blue china.

There he gave some orders to Mrs. Deacon, obtained a cigarette, and passed back along the passage to a small, cosy, panelled room at the end of the house – the room wherein he wrote those mystery stories which held the world enthralled.

It was a pretty, restful place, with a moss-green carpet, green-covered chairs, several cases filled to overflowing with books, and a great writing-table set in the window. On the mantelshelf were many autographed portraits of Continental celebrities, while on the walls were one or two little gems of antique art which he had picked up on his erratic wanderings. Over the writing-table was a barometer and a storm-glass, while to the left a cosy corner extended round to the fireplace.

He lit his cigarette, then walking across to a small square oaken door let into the wall beside the fireplace, he opened it with a key. This had been an oven before the transformation of three cottages into a weekend residence, and on opening it there was displayed the dark-green door of a safe. This he quickly opened with another key, and after slight search took out a small ledger covered with dark-red leather.

Then glancing at some numerals upon a piece of paper he took from his vest pocket, he turned them up in the index, and with another volume open upon his blotting-pad, he settled himself to read the record written there in a small, round hand. The numbers were those upon the back of the old *carte-de-visite* which had interested him so keenly, and the statement he was reading was, from the expression upon his countenance, an amazing one.

From time to time he scribbled memoranda upon the scrap of paper, now and then pausing as though to recall the past. Then, when he had finished, he laughed softly to himself, and, closing the book, replaced it in the safe and shut the oaken door. By the inspection of that secret entry he had learnt much regarding that man who posed as a doctor in Pimlico.

He sat back in his writing-chair and puffed thoughtfully at his cigarette. Then he turned his attention to a pile of letters addressed to him as "Mr. Maltwood," and made some scribbled replies until Mrs. Deacon entered to announce that his luncheon was ready.

When he went back to the quaint, old-fashioned dining-room and seated himself, he said: "I'm going back by the five-eighteen, and I dare say I shan't return for quite a month or perhaps six weeks. Here's a cheque for ten pounds to pay these little bills." And he commenced his solitary meal.

"You haven't been here much this summer, sir," remarked the good woman. "In Idsworth they think you've quite deserted us – Mr. Barnes was only saying so last week. They're all so glad to see you down here, sir."

"That's very good of them, Mrs. Deacon," he laughed. "I, too, only wish I could spend more time here. I love the country, and I'm never so happy as when wandering in Idsworth woods."

And then he asked her to tell him the village gossip while she waited at his table.

After luncheon he put on a rough suit and, taking his stout holly stick, went for a ramble through the great woods he loved so well, where the trees were tinted by autumn and the pheasants were strong upon the wing.

He found Findlay, one of the keepers, and walked with him for an hour as far as the Roman camp, where alone he sat down upon a felled tree and, with his gaze fixed across the distant hills towards the sea, pondered deeply. He loved his modest country cottage, and he loved those quiet, homely Dorsetshire folk around him. Yet such a wanderer was he that only a few months each year – the months he wrote those wonderful romances of his – could he spend in that old-fashioned cottage which he had rendered the very acme of cosiness and comfort.

At half-past four the rickety station fly called for him, and later he left by the express which took him to Waterloo and his club in time for dinner.

And so once again he changed his identity from John Maltwood, busy man of business, to Walter Fetherston, novelist and traveller.

The seriousness of what was in progress was now plain to him. He had long been filled with strong suspicions, and these suspicions had been confirmed both by Enid's statements and his own observations; therefore he was already alert and watchful.

At ten o'clock he went to his gloomy chambers for an hour, and then strolled forth to the Vauxhall Bridge Road, and remained vigilant outside the doctor's house until nearly two.

He noted those who came and went – two men who called before midnight, and were evidently foreigners. They came separately, remained about half an hour, and then Weirmarsh himself let them out, shaking hands with them effusively.

Suddenly a taxicab drove up, and from it Sir Hugh, in black overcoat and opera hat, stepped out and was at once admitted, the taxi driving off. Walter, as he paced up and down the pavement outside, would have given much to know what was transpiring within.

Had he been able to glance inside that shabby little back room he would have witnessed a strange scene - Sir Hugh, the gallant old soldier, crushed and humiliated by the man who practised medicine, and who called himself Weirmarsh.

"I had only just come in from the theatre when you telephoned me," Sir Hugh said sharply on entering. "I am sorry I could make no appointment today, but I was at the War Office all the morning, lunched at the Carlton, and was afterwards quite full up."

"There was no immediate hurry, Sir Hugh," responded the doctor with a pleasant smile. "I quite understand that your many social engagements prevented you from seeing me. I should have been round at noon, only I was called out to an urgent case. Therefore no apology is needed - by either of us." Then, after a pause, he looked sharply at the man seated before him and asked: "I presume you have reconsidered your decision, General, and will carry out my request?"

"No, I have not decided to do that," was the old fellow's firm answer. "It's too dangerous an exploit - far too dangerous. Besides, it means ruin."

"My dear sir," remarked the doctor, "you are viewing the matter in quite a wrong light. There will be no suspicion providing you exercise due caution."

"And what would be the use of that, pray, when my secret will not be mine alone? It is already known to half a dozen other persons - your friends - any of whom might give me away."

"It will not be known until afterwards - when you are safe.

Therefore, there will be absolutely no risk," the doctor assured him.

The other, however, was no fool, and was still unconvinced. He knew well that to carry out the request made by Weirmarsh involved considerable risk.

The doctor spoke quietly, but very firmly. In his demands he was always inexorable. He had already hinted at the disaster which might fall upon Sir Hugh if he refused to obey. Weirmarsh was, the general knew from bitter experience, not a man to be trifled with.

Completely and irrevocably he was in this man's hands. During the past twenty-four hours the grave old fellow, who had faced death a hundred times, had passed through a crisis of agony and despair. He hated himself, and would even have welcomed death, would have courted it at his own hands, had not these jeers of the doctor's rung in his ears. And, after all, he had decided that suicide was only a coward's death. The man who takes his own life to avoid exposure is always despised by his friends.

So he had lived, and had come down there in response to the doctor's request over the telephone, resolved to face the music, if for the last time.

He sat in the shabby old armchair and firmly refused to carry out the doctor's suggestion. But Weirmarsh, with his innate cunning, presented to him a picture of exposure and degradation which held him horrified.

"I should have thought, Sir Hugh, that in face of what must inevitably result you would not risk exposure," he said. "Of course, it lies with you entirely," he added with an unconcerned air.

"I'm thinking of my family," the old officer said slowly.

"Of the disgrace if the truth were known, eh?"

"No; of the suspicion, nay, ruin and imprisonment, that would fall upon another person," replied Sir Hugh.

"No suspicion can be aroused if you are careful, I repeat," exclaimed Weirmarsh impatiently. "Not a breath of suspicion has ever fallen upon you up to the present, has it? No, because you have exercised foresight and have followed to the letter the plans I made. I ask you, when you have followed my advice have you ever gone wrong - have you ever taken one false step?"

"Never - since the first," replied the old soldier in a hard, bitter tone.

"Then I urge you to continue to follow the advice I give you, namely, to agree to the terms."

"And who will be aware of the matter?"

"Only myself," was Weirmarsh's reply. "And I think that you may trust a secret with me?"

The old man made no reply, and the crafty doctor wondered whether by silence he very reluctantly gave his consent.

CHAPTER VIII

PAUL LE PONTOIS

There is in the far north-west of France a broad, white highway which runs from Châlons, crosses the green Meuse valley, mounts the steep, high, tree-fringed lands of the Côtes Lorraines, and goes almost straight as an arrow across what was, before the war, the German frontier at Mars-la-Tour into quaint old Metz, that town with ancient streets, musical chimes, and sad monument to Frenchmen who fell in the disastrous never-to-be-forgotten war of '70.

This road has ever been one of the most strongly guarded highways in the world, for, between the Moselle, at Metz, and the Meuse, the country is a flat plain smiling under cultivation, with vines and cornfields everywhere, and comfortable little homesteads of the peasantry. This was once the great battlefield whereon Gravelotte was fought long ago, and where the Prussians swept back the French like chaff before the wind, and where France, later on, defeated the Crown Prince's army. The peasants, in ploughing, daily turn up a rusty bayonet, a rotting gun-stock, a skull, a thigh-bone, or some other hideous relic of those black days; while the old men in their blouses sit of nights smoking and telling thrilling stories of the ferocity of that helmeted enemy from yonder across the winding Moselle. In recent days it has been again devastated by the great world war, as its gaunt ruins mutely tell.

That road, with its long line of poplars, after crossing the ante-war

French border, runs straight for twenty kilomètres towards the abrupt range of high hills which form the natural frontier of France, and then, at Haudiomont, enters a narrow pass, over twelve kilomètres long, before it reaches the broad valley of the Meuse. This pass was, before 1914, one of the four principal gateways into France from Germany. The others are all within a short distance, fifteen kilomètres or so – at Commercy, which is an important sous-prefecture, at Apremont, and at Eix. All have ever been strongly guarded, but that at Haudiomont was most impregnable of them all.

Before 1914 great forts in which were mounted the most modern and the most destructive artillery ever devised by man, commanded the whole country far beyond the Moselle into Germany. Every hill-top bristled with them, smaller batteries were in every coign of vantage, while those narrow mountain passes could also be closed at any moment by being blown up when the signal was given against the Hun invaders.

On the German side were many fortresses, but none was so strong as these, for the efforts of the French Ministry of War had, ever since the fall of Napoleon III., been directed towards rendering the Côtes Lorraines impassable.

As one stands upon the road outside the tiny hamlet of Harville – a quaint but half-destroyed little place consisting of one long street of ruined whitewashed houses – and looks towards the hills eastward, low concrete walls can be seen, half hidden, but speaking mutely of the withering storm of shell that had, in 1914, burst from them and swept the land.

Much can be seen of that chain of damaged fortresses, and the details of most of them are now known. Of those great ugly fortifications at Moulainville – the Belrupt Fort, which overlooks the Meuse; the Daumaumont, commanding the road from Conflans to

Azannes; the Paroches, which stands directly over the highway from the Moselle at Moussin – we have heard valiant stories, how the brave French defended them against the armies of the Crown Prince.

It was not upon these, however, that the French Army relied when, in August, 1914, the clash of war resounded along that pleasant fertile valley, where the sun seems ever to shine and the crops never fail. Hidden away from the sight of passers-by upon the roads, protected from sight by lines of sentries night and day, and unapproachable, save by those immediately connected with them, were the secret defences, huge forts with long-range ordnance, which rose, fired, and disappeared again, offering no mark for the enemy. Constructed in strictest secrecy, there were a dozen of such fortresses, the true details of which the Huns vainly endeavoured to learn while they were war-plotting. Many a spy of the Kaiser had tried to pry there and had been arrested and sentenced to a long term of imprisonment.

Those defences, placed at intervals along the chain of hills right from Apremont away to Bezonvaux, had been the greatest secret which France possessed.

Within three kilomètres of the mouth of the pass at Haudiomont, at a short distance from the road and at the edge of a wood, stood the ancient Château de Lérouville, a small picturesque place of the days of Louis XIV, with pretty lawns and old-world gardens – a château only in the sense of being a country house and the residence of Paul Le Pontois, once a captain in the French Army, but now retired.

Shut off from the road by a high old wall, with great iron gates, it was approached by a wide carriage-drive through a well-kept flower-garden to a long *terrasse* which ran the whole length of the house, and whereon, in summer, it was the habit of the family to take their meals.

Upon this veranda, one morning about ten days after the dinner party at Hill Street, Sir Hugh, in a suit of light grey tweed, was standing chatting with his son-in-law, a tall, brown-bearded, soldierly-looking man.

The autumn sun shone brightly over the rich vinelands, beyond which stretched what was once the German Empire.

Madame Le Pontois, a slim, dark-eyed, good-looking woman of thirty, was still at table in the *salle-à-manger*, finishing her breakfast in the English style with little Ninette, a pretty blue-eyed child of nine, whose hair was tied on the top with wide white ribbon, and who spoke English quite well.

Her husband and her father had gone out upon the *terrasse* to have their cigarettes prior to their walk up the steep hillside to the fortress.

Life in that rural district possessed few amusements outside the military circle, though Paul Le Pontois was a civilian and lived upon the product of the wine-lands of his estate. There were tennis parties, "fif' o'clocks," croquet and bridge-playing in the various military houses around, but beyond that – nothing. They were too far from a big town ever to go there for recreation. Metz they seldom went to, and with Paris far off, Madame Le Pontois was quite content, just as she had been when Paul had been stationed in stifling Constantine, away in the interior of Algeria.

But she never complained. Devoted to her husband and to her laughing, bright-eyed child, she loved the open-air life of the country, and with such a commodious and picturesque house, one of the best in the district, she thoroughly enjoyed every hour of her life. Paul possessed a private income of fifty thousand francs, or nearly two thousand pounds a year, therefore he was better off than the average run of post-war men.

He was a handsome, distinguished-looking man. As he lolled against the railing of the *terrasse*, gay with ivy-leaf geraniums, lazily smoking his cigarette and laughing lightly with his father-in-law, he presented a typical picture of the debonair Frenchman of the boulevards – elegance combined with soldierly smartness.

He had seen service in Tonquin, in Algeria, on the French Congo and in the Argonne, and now his old company garrisoned Haudiomont, one of those forts of enormous strength, which commanded the gate of France, and had never been taken by the Crown Prince's army.

"No," he was laughing, speaking in good English, "you in England, my dear beaupère, do not yet realise the dangers of the future. Happily for you, perhaps, because you have the barrier of the sea. Your writers used to speak of your 'tight little island.' But I do not see much of that in London journals now. Airships and aeroplanes have altered all that."

"But you in France are always on the alert?"

"Certainly. We have our new guns – terrible weapons they are – at St. Mihiel and at Mouilly, and also in other forts in what was once German territory," was Paul's reply. "The Huns – who, after peace, are preparing for another war, have a Krupp gun for the same purpose, but at its trial a few weeks ago at Pferzheim it was an utter failure. A certain lieutenant was present at the trial, disguised as a German peasant. He saw it all, returned here, and made an exhaustive report to Paris."

"You do not believe in this peace, and in the sincerity of the enemy, eh?" asked Sir Hugh, with his hands thrust deep into his trousers pockets.

"Certainly not," was Paul's prompt reply. "I am no longer in the army, but it seems to me that to repair the damage done by the Kaiser's freak performances in the international arena, quite a number of national committees must be constituted under the auspices of the German Government. There are the Anglo-German, the Austro-German, the American-German and the Canadian-German committees, all to be formed in their respective countries for the promotion of friendship and better relations. But I tell you, Sir Hugh, that we in France know well that the imposing names at the head of these committees are but too often on the secret pay-rolls of the Wilhelmstrasse, and the honesty and sincerity of the finely-worded manifestations of Hun friendship and goodwill appearing above their signatures are generally nothing but mere blinds intended to hoodwink statesmen and public opinion. Germany has, just as she had before the war, her paid friends everywhere," he added, looking the general full in the face. "In all classes of society are to be found the secret agents of the Fatherland – men who are base traitors to their own monarch and to their own land."

"Let us go in. They are waiting for us. We are not interested in espionage, either of us, are we?"

"No," laughed Paul. "When I was in the army we heard a lot of this, but all that is of the past – thanks to Heaven. There are other crimes in the world just as bad, alas! As that of treachery to one's country."

CHAPTER IX

THE LITTLE OLD FRENCHWOMAN

Although Sir Hugh had on frequent occasions been the guest of his son-in-law at the pretty Château de Lérouville, he had never expressed a wish, until the previous evening, to enter the Fortress of Haudiomont.

As a military man he knew well how zealously the secrets of all fortresses are guarded.

When, on the previous evening, Le Pontois had declared that it would be an easy matter for him to be granted a view of that great stronghold hidden away among the hill-tops, he had remarked: "Of course, my dear Paul, I would not for a moment dream of putting you into any awkward position. Remember, I am an alien here, and a soldier also! I haven't any desire to see the place."

"Oh, there is no question of that so far as you are concerned, Sir Hugh," Paul had declared with a light laugh. "The Commandant, who, of course, knows you, asked me a month ago to bring you up next time you visited us. He wished to make your acquaintance. In view of the recent war our people are nowadays no longer afraid of England, you know!"

So the visit had been arranged, and Sir Hugh was to take his *déjeuner* up at the fort.

That day Blanche, with Enid, who had accompanied her stepfather, drove the runabout car up the valley to the little station at Dieue-sur-Meuse, and took the train thence to Commercy, where

Blanche wished to do some shopping.

So, when the two men had left to ascend the steep hillside, where the great fortress lay concealed, Blanche, who had by long residence in France become almost a Frenchwoman, kissed little Ninette *au revoir*, climbed into the car, and, taking the wheel, drove Enid and Jean, the servant, who, as a soldier, had served Paul during the war, away along the winding valley.

As they went along they passed a battalion of the 113th Regiment of the Line, heavy with their knapsacks, their red trousers dusty, returning from the long morning march, and singing as they went that very old regimental ditty which every soldier of France knows so well:

"La Noire est fille du cannon
Qui se fout du qu'en dira-t-on.
Nous nous foutons de ses vertus,
Puisqu'elle a les tétons pointus.
    Voilà pourquoi nous la chantons:
    Vive la Noire et ses tétons!"

And as they passed the ladies the officer saluted. They were, Blanche explained, on their way back to the great camp at Jarny.

Bugles were sounding among the hills, while ever and anon came the low boom of distant artillery at practice away in the direction of Vigneulles-les-Hattonchatel, the headquarters of the sub-division of that military region.

It was Enid's first visit, and the activity about her surprised her. Besides, the officers were extremely good-looking.

Presently they approached a battery of artillery on the march, with their rumbling guns and grey ammunition wagons, raising a cloud of dust as they advanced.

Blanche pulled the car up at the side of the road to allow them to pass, and as she did so a tall, smartly-groomed major rode up to her, and, saluting, exclaimed in French, "Bon jour, Madame! I intended to call upon you this morning. My wife has heard that you have the general, your father, visiting you, and we wanted to know if you would all come and take dinner with us tomorrow night?"

"I'm sure we'd be most delighted," replied Paul's wife, at the same time introducing Enid to Major Delagrange.

"My father has gone up to the fort with my husband," Blanche added, bending over from the car.

"Ah, then I shall meet them at noon," replied the smart officer, backing his bay horse. "And you ladies are going out for a run, eh? Beautiful morning! We've been out manœuvring since six!"

Blanche explained that they were on a shopping expedition to Commercy, and then, saluting, Delagrange set spurs into his horse and galloped away after the retreating battery.

"That man's wife is one of my best friends. She speaks English very well, and is quite a good sort. Delagrange and Paul were in Tonquin together and are great friends."

"I suppose you are never very dull here, with so much always going on?" Enid remarked. "Why anyone would believe that a war was actually in progress!"

"This post of Eastern France never sleeps, my dear," was Madame's reply. "While you in England remain secure in your island, we here never know when trouble may again arise. Therefore, we are always preparing – and at the same time always prepared."

"It must be most exciting," declared the girl, "to live in such uncertainty. Is the danger so very real, then?" she asked. "Father generally pooh-poohs the notion of there being any further trouble with Germany."

"I know," was Blanche's answer. "He has been sceptical hitherto. He is always suspicious of the Boche!"

They had driven up to the little wayside station, and, giving the car over to Jean with instructions to meet the five-forty train, they entered a first-class compartment.

Between Dieue and Commercy the railway follows the course of the Meuse the whole way, winding up a narrow, fertile valley, the hills of which on the right, which once were swept by the enemy's shells and completely devastated, were all strongly fortified with great guns commanding the plain that lies between the Meuse and the Moselle.

They were passing through one of the most interesting districts in all France – that quiet, fertile valley where stood peaceful, prosperous homesteads, and where the sheep were once more calmly grazing – the valley which for four years was so strongly contested, and where every village had been more or less destroyed.

At the headquarters of the Sixth Army Corps of France much was known, much that was still alarming. It was that knowledge which urged on those ever active military preparations, for placing that district of France that had been ravaged by the Hun in the Great War in a state of complete fortification as a second line of defence should trouble again arise.

Thoughts such as these arose in Enid's mind as she sat in silence looking forth upon the panorama of green hills and winding stream as they slowly approached the quaint town of Commercy.

Arrived there, the pair lunched at the old-fashioned Hôtel de Paris, under the shadow of the great château, once the residence of the Dukes de Lorraine, and much damaged in the war, but nowadays a hive of activity as an infantry barracks. And afterwards they went forth to do their shopping in the busy little Rue de la République, not forgetting to buy a box of "madeleines." As shortbread is the specialty of Edinburgh, as butterscotch is that of Doncaster, "maids-of-honour" that of Richmond, and strawberry jam that of Bar-le-Duc, so are "madeleines" the special cakes of Commercy.

The town was full of officers and soldiers. In every café officers were smoking cigarettes and gossiping after their *déjeuner*, while ever and anon bugles sounded, and there was the clang and clatter of military movement.

As the two ladies approached the big bronze statue of Dom Calmet, the historian, they passed a small café. Suddenly a man idling within over a newspaper sprang to his feet in surprise, and next second drew back as if in fear of observation.

It was Walter Fetherston. He had come up from Nancy that morning, and had since occupied the time in strolling about seeing the sights of the little place.

His surprise at seeing Enid was very great. He knew that she was staying in the vicinity, but had never expected to see her so quickly.

The lady who accompanied her he guessed to be her stepsister; indeed, he had seen a photograph of her at Hill Street. Had Enid been alone, he would have rushed forth to greet her; but he had no desire at the moment that his presence should be known to Madame Le Pontois. He was there to watch, and to meet Enid – but alone.

So after a few moments he cautiously went forth from the café, and followed the two ladies at a respectful distance, until he saw them complete their purchases and afterwards enter the station to return home.

On his return to the hotel he made many inquiries of monsieur the proprietor concerning the distance to Haudiomont, and learned a good deal about the military works there which was of the greatest interest. The hotel-keeper, a stout Alsatian, was a talkative person, and told Walter nearly all he wished to know.

Since leaving Charing Cross five days before he had been ever active. On his arrival in Paris he had gone to the apartment of Colonel Maynard, the British military attaché, and spent the evening with him. Then, at one o'clock next morning, he had hurriedly taken his bag and left for Dijon, where at noon he had been met in the Café de la Rotonde by a little wizen-faced old Frenchwoman in seedy black, who had travelled for two days and nights in order to meet him.

Together they had walked out on that unfrequented road beyond the Place Darcy, chatting confidentially as they went, the old lady speaking emphatically and with many gesticulations as they walked.

Truth to tell, this insignificant-looking person was a woman of many secrets. She was a "friend" of the Sûreté Générale in Paris. She lived, and lived well, in a pretty apartment in Paris upon the handsome salary which she received regularly each quarter. But she was seldom at home. Like Walter, her days were spent travelling hither and thither across Europe.

It would surprise the public if it were aware of the truth – the truth of how, in every country in Europe, there are secret female agents of police who (for a monetary consideration, of course) keep watch in great centres where the presence of a man would be suspected.

This secret police service is distinctly apart from the detective service. The female police agent in all countries works independently, at the orders of the Director of Criminal Investigation, and is known to him and his immediate staff.

Whatever information that wrinkled-faced old Frenchwoman in shabby black had imparted to Fetherston it was of an entirely confidential character. It, however, caused him to leave her about three o'clock, hurry to the Gare Porte-Neuve, and, after hastily swallowing a liqueur of brandy in the buffet, depart for Langres.

Thence he had travelled to Nancy, where he had taken up quarters at the Grand Hotel in the Place Stanislas, and had there remained for two days in order to rest.

He would not have idled those autumn days away so lazily, even though he so urgently required rest after that rapid travelling, had he but known that the person who occupied the next room to his – that middle-aged commercial traveller – an entirely inoffensive person who possessed a red beard, and who had given the name of Jules Dequanter, and his nationality as Belgian, native of Liège – was none other than Gustav Heureux, the man who had been recalled from New York by the evasive doctor of Pimlico.

And further, Fetherston, notwithstanding his acuteness in observation, was in blissful ignorance, as he strolled back from the station at Commercy, up the old-world street, that a short distance behind him, carefully watching all his movements, was the man Joseph Blot himself – the man known in dingy Pimlico as Dr. Weirmarsh.

CHAPTER X

IF ANYONE KNEW

Sir Hugh Elcombe spent a most interesting and instructive day within the Fortress of Haudiomont. He really did not want to go. The visit bored him. The world was at peace, and there was no incentive to espionage as there had been in pre-war days.

General Henri Molon, the commandant, greeted him cordially and himself showed him over a portion of the post-war defences which were kept such a strict secret from everyone. The general did not, however, show his distinguished guest everything. Such things as the new anti-aircraft gun, the exact disposition of the huge mines placed in the valley between there and Rozellier, so that at a given signal both road and railway tracks could be destroyed, he did not point out. There were other matters to which the smart, grey-haired, old French general deemed it unwise to refer, even though his visitor might be a high official of a friendly Power.

Sir Hugh noticed all this and smiled inwardly. He wandered about the bomb-proof case-mates hewn out of the solid rock, caring nothing for the number and calibre of the guns, their armoured protection, or the chart-like diagrams upon the walls, ranges and the like.

"What a glorious evening!" Paul was saying as, at sunset, they set their faces towards the valley beyond which lay shattered Germany. That peaceful land, the theatre of the recent war, lay bathed in the soft rose of the autumn afterglow, while the bright clearness of the sky, pale-green and gold, foretold a frost.

"Yes, splendid!" responded his father-in-law mechanically; but he was thinking of something far more serious than the beauties of the western sky. He was thinking of the grip in which he was held by the doctor of Pimlico. At any moment, if he cared to collapse, he could make ten thousand pounds in a single day. The career of many a man has been blasted for ever by the utterance of cruel untruths or the repetition of vague suspicions. Was his son-in-law, Le Pontois, in jeopardy? He could not think that he was. How could the truth come out? Sir Hugh asked himself. It never had before – though his friend had made a million sterling, and there was no reason whatever why it should come out now. He had tested Weirmarsh thoroughly, and knew him to be a man to be trusted.

As he strolled on at his son-in-law's side, chatting to him, he was full of anxiety as to the future. He had left England, it was true. He had defied the doctor. But the latter had been inexorable. If he continued in his defiance, then ruin must inevitably come to him.

Blanche and Enid had already returned, and at dusk all four sat down to dinner together with little Ninette, for whom "Aunt Enid" had brought a new doll which had given the child the greatest delight.

The meal ended, the bridge-table was set in the pretty salon adjoining, and several games were played until Sir Hugh, pleading fatigue, at last ascended to his room.

Within, he locked the door and cast himself into a chair before the big log fire to think.

That day had indeed been a strenuous one – strenuous for any man. So occupied had been his brain that he scarcely recollected any conversations with those smart debonair officers to whom Paul had introduced him.

As he sat there he closed his eyes, and before him arose visions of interviews in dingy offices in London, one of them behind Soho Square.

For a full hour he sat there immovable as a statue, reflecting, ever recalling the details of those events.

Suddenly he sprang to his feet with clenched hands.

"My God!" he cried, his teeth set and countenance pale. "My God! If anybody ever knew the truth!"

He crossed to the window, drew aside the blind, and looked out upon the moonlit plains.

Below, his daughter was still playing the piano and singing an old English ballad.

"She's happy, ah! My dear Blanche!" the old man murmured between his teeth. "But if suspicion falls upon me? Ah! If it does; then it means ruin to them both – ruin because of a dastardly action of mine!"

He returned unsteadily to his chair, and sat staring straight into the embers, his hands to his hot, fevered brow. More than once he sighed – sighed heavily, as a man when fettered and compelled to act against his better nature.

Again he heard his daughter's voice below, now singing a gay little French chanson, a song of the café chantant and of the Paris boulevards.

In a flash there recurred to him every incident of those dramatic interviews with the Mephistophelean doctor. He would at that moment have given his very soul to be free of that calm, clever, insinuating man who, while providing him with a handsome, even unlimited income, yet at the same time held him irrevocably in the hollow of his hand.

He, a brilliant British soldier with a magnificent record, honoured by his sovereign, was, after all, but a tool of that obscure doctor, the man who had come into his life to rescue him from bankruptcy and disgrace.

When he reflected he bit his lip in despair. Yet there was no way out – *none!* Weirmarsh had really been most generous. The cosy house in

Hill Street, the smart little entertainments which his wife gave, the bit of shooting he rented up in the Highlands, were all paid for with the money which the doctor handed him in Treasury notes with such regularity.

Yes, Weirmarsh was generous, but he was nevertheless exacting, terribly exacting. His will was the will of others.

The blazing logs had died down to a red mass, the voice of Blanche had ceased. He had heard footsteps an hour ago in the corridor outside, and knew that the family had retired. There was not a sound. All were asleep, save the sentries high upon that hidden fortress. Again the old general sighed wearily. His grey face now wore an expression of resignation. He had thought it all out, and saw that to resist and refuse would only spell ruin for both himself and his family. He had but himself to blame after all. He had taken one false step, and he had been held inexorably to his contract.

So he yawned wearily, rose, stretched himself, and then, pacing the room twice, at last turned up the lamp and placed it upon the small writing-table at the foot of the bed. Afterwards he took from his suitcase a quire of ruled foolscap paper and a fountain pen, and, seating himself, sat for some time with his head in his hands deep in thought. Suddenly the clock in the big hall below chimed two upon its peal of silvery bells. This aroused him, and, taking up his pen, he began to write.

Ever and anon as he wrote he sat back and reflected.

Hour after hour he sat there, bent to the table, his pen rapidly travelling over the paper. He wrote down many figures and was making calculations.

At half-past four he put down his pen. The sum was not complete, but it was one which he knew would end his career and bring him into the dock of a criminal court, and Weirmarsh and others would stand beside him.

All this he had done in entire ignorance of one startling fact – namely, that outside his window for the past hour a dark figure had been standing in an insecure position upon the lead guttering of the wing of the château which ran out at right angles, leaning forward and peering in between the blind and the window-frame, watching with interest all that had been in progress.

CHAPTER XI

CONCERNS THE PAST

One evening, a few days after Sir Hugh had paid another visit to Haudiomont, he was smoking with Paul prior to retiring to bed when the conversation drifted upon money matters – some investment he had made in England in his wife's name.

Paul had allowed his father-in-law to handle some of his money in England, for Sir Hugh was very friendly with a man named Hewett in the City, who had on several occasions put him on good things.

Indeed, just before Sir Hugh had left London he had had a wire from Paul to sell some shares at a big profit, and he had brought over the proceeds in Treasury notes, quite a respectable sum. There had been a matter of concealing certain payments, Sir Hugh explained, and that was why he had brought over the money instead of a cheque.

As they were chatting Sir Hugh, referring to the transaction, said:

"Hewett suggested that I should have it in notes – four five-hundred Bank of England ones and the rest in Treasury notes."

"I sent them to the Crédit Lyonnais a few days ago," replied his son-in-law. "Really, Sir Hugh, you did a most excellent bit of business with Hewett. I hope you profited yourself."

"Yes, a little bit," laughed the old general. "Can't complain, you know. I'm glad you've sent the notes to the bank. It was a big sum to keep in the house here."

"Yes, I see only today they've credited me with them," was his reply.

"I hope you can induce Hewett to do a bit more for us. Those aeroplane shares are still going up, I see by the London papers."

"And they'll continue to do so, my dear Paul," was the reply. "But those Bolivian four per cents of yours I'd sell if I were you. They'll never be higher."

"You don't think so?"

"Hewett warned me. He told me to tell you. Of course, you're richer than I am, and can afford to keep them. Only I warn you."

"Very well," replied the younger man, "when you get back, sell them, will you?"

And Sir Hugh promised that he would give instructions to that effect.

"Really, my dear beau-père," Paul said, "you've been an awfully good friend to me. Since I left the army I've made quite a big sum out of my speculations in London."

"And mostly paid with English notes, eh?" laughed the elder man.

"Yes. Just let me see." And, taking a piece of paper, he sat down at the writing-table and made some quick calculations of various sums. Upon one side he placed the money he had invested, and on the other the profits, at last striking a balance at the end. Then he told the general the figure.

"Quite good," declared Sir Hugh. "I'm only too glad, my dear Paul, to be of any assistance to you. I fear you are vegetating here. But as long as your wife doesn't mind it, what matters?"

"Blanche loves this country - which is fortunate, seeing that I have this big place to attend to." And as he said this he rose, screwed up the sheet of thin note-paper, and tossed it into the waste-paper basket.

The pair separated presently, and Sir Hugh went to his room. He was eager and anxious to get away and return to London, but there was a difficulty. Enid, who had lately taken up amateur theatricals, had accepted an invitation to play in a comedy to be given at General Molon's house in a week's time in aid of the Croix Rouge. Therefore he was compelled to remain on her account.

On the following afternoon Blanche drove him in her car through the beautiful Bois de Hermeville, glorious in its autumn gold, down to the quaint old village of Warcq, to take "fif o'clock" at the château with the Countess de Pierrepont, Paul's widowed aunt.

Enid had pleaded a headache, but as soon as the car had driven away she roused herself, and, ascending to her room, put on strong country boots and a leather-hemmed golf skirt, and, taking a stick, set forth down the high road lined with poplars in the direction of Mars-la-Tour.

About a mile from Lérouville she came to the cross-roads, the one to the south leading over the hills to Vigneulles, while the one to the north joined the highway to Longuyon. For a moment she paused, then turning into the latter road, which at that point was little more than a byway, hurried on until she came to the fringe of a wood, where, upon her approach, a man in dark grey tweeds came forth to meet her with swinging gait.

It was Walter Fetherston.

He strode quickly in her direction, and when they met he held her small hand in his and for a moment gazed into her dark eyes without uttering a word.

"At last!" he cried. "I was afraid that you had not received my message – that it might have been intercepted."

"I got it early this morning," was her reply, her cheeks flushing with pleasure; "but I was unable to get away before my father and Blanche went out. They pressed me to go with them, so I had to plead a headache."

"I am so glad we've met," Fetherston said. "I have been here in the vicinity for days, yet I feared to come near you lest your father should recognise me."

"But why are you here?" she inquired, strolling slowly at his side. "I thought you were in London."

"I'm seldom in London," he responded. "Nowadays I am constantly on the move."

"Travelling in search of fresh material for your books, I suppose? I read in a paper the other day that you never describe a place in your stories without first visiting it. If so, you must travel a great deal," the girl remarked.

"I do," he answered briefly. "And very often I travel quickly."

"But why are you here?"

"For several reasons – the chief being to see you, Enid."

For a moment the girl did not reply. This man's movements so often mystified her. He seemed ubiquitous. In one single fortnight he had sent her letters from Paris, Stockholm, Hamburg, Vienna and Constanza. His huge circle of friends was unequalled. In almost every city on the Continent he knew somebody, and he was a perfect encyclopædia of travel. His strange reticence, however, always increased the mystery surrounding him. Those vague whispers concerning him had reached her ears, and she often wondered whether half she heard concerning him was true.

If a man prefers not to speak of himself or of his doings, his enemies will soon invent some tale of their own. And thus it was in Walter's case. Men had uttered foul calumnies concerning him merely because they believed him to be eccentric and unsociable.

But Enid Orlebar, though she somehow held him in suspicion, nevertheless liked him. In certain moods he possessed that dash and devil-may-care air which pleases most women, providing the man is a cosmopolitan.

He was ever courteous, ever solicitous for her welfare.

She had known he loved her ever since they had first met. Indeed, has he not told her so?

As they walked together down that grass-grown byway through the wood, where the brown leaves were floating down with every gust, she glanced into his pale, dark, serious face and wondered. In her nostrils was the autumn perfume of the woods, and as they strode forward in silence a rabbit scuttled from their path.

"You are, no doubt, surprised that I am here," he commenced at last. "But it is in your interests, Enid."

"In my interests?" she echoed. "Why?"

"Regarding the secret relations between your stepfather and Doctor Weirmarsh," he answered.

"That same question we've discussed before," she said. "The doctor is attending to his practice in Pimlico; he does not concern us here."

"I fear that he does," was Fetherston's quiet response. "That man holds your stepfather's future in his hand."

"How – how can he?"

"By the same force by which he holds that indescribable influence over you."

"You believe, then, that he possesses some occult power?"

"Not at all. His power is the power which every evil man possesses. And as far as my observation goes, I can detect that Sir Hugh has fallen into some trap which has been cunningly prepared for him."

Enid gasped and her countenance blanched.

"You believe, then, that those consultations I have had with the doctor are at his own instigation?"

"Most certainly. Sir Hugh hates Weirmarsh, but, fearing exposure, he must obey the fellow's will."

"But cannot you discover the truth?" asked the girl eagerly. "Cannot we free my stepfather? He's such a dear old fellow, and is always so good and kind to my mother and myself."

"That is exactly my object in asking you to meet me here, Enid," said the novelist, his countenance still thoughtful and serious.

"How can I assist?" she asked quickly. "Only explain, and I will act upon any suggestion you may make."

"You can assist by giving me answers to certain questions," was his slow reply. The inquiry was delicate and difficult to pursue without arousing the girl's suspicions as to the exact situation and the hideous scandal in progress.

"What do you wish to know?" she asked in some surprise, for she saw by his countenance that he was deeply in earnest.

"Well," he said, with some little hesitation, glancing at her pale, handsome face as he walked by her side, "I fear you may think me too inquisitive - that the questions I'm going to ask are out of sheer curiosity."

"I shall not if by replying I can assist my stepfather to escape from that man's thraldom."

He was silent for a moment; then he said slowly: "I think Sir Hugh was in command of a big training camp in Norfolk early in the war, was he not?"

"Yes. I went with him, and we stayed for about three months at the King's Head at Beccles."

"And during the time you were at the King's Head, did the doctor ever visit Sir Hugh?"

"Yes; the doctor stayed several times at the Royal at Lowestoft. We both motored over on several occasions and dined with him. Doctor Weirmarsh was not well, so he had gone to the east coast for a change."

"And he also came over to Beccles to see your stepfather?"

"Yes; twice, or perhaps three times. One evening after dinner, I remember, they left the hotel and went for a long walk together. I recollect it well, for I had been out all day and had a bad headache. Therefore, the doctor went along to the chemist's on his way out and ordered me a draught."

"You took it?"

"Yes; and I went to sleep almost immediately, and did not wake up till very late next morning," she replied.

"You recollect, too, a certain man named Bellairs?"

"Ah, yes!" she sighed. "How very sad it was! Poor Captain Bellairs was a great favourite of the general, and served on his staff."

"He was with him in the Boer War, was he not?"

"Yes. But how do you know all this?" asked the girl, looking curiously at her questioner and turning slightly paler.

"Well," he replied evasively, "I – I've been told so, and wished to know whether it was a fact. You and he were friends, eh?" he asked after a pause.

For a moment the girl did not reply. A flood of sad memories swept through her mind at the mention of Harry Bellairs.

"Yes," she replied, "we were great friends. He took me to concerts and matinées in town sometimes. Sir Hugh always said he was a man bound to make his mark. He had earned his DSO with the French at Mons and was twice mentioned in dispatches."

"And you, Enid," he said, still speaking very slowly, his dark eyes fixed upon hers, "you would probably have consented to become Mrs. Bellairs had he lived to ask you? Tell me the truth."

Her eyes were cast down; he saw in them the light of unshed tears.

"Pardon me for referring to such a painful subject," he hastened to say, "but it is imperative."

"I thought that you were – were unaware of the sad affair," she faltered.

"So I was until quite recently," he replied. "I know how deeply it must pain you to speak of it, but will you please explain to me the actual facts? I know that you are better acquainted with them than anyone else."

"The facts of poor Harry's death," she repeated hoarsely, as though speaking to herself. "Why recall them? Oh! Why recall them?"

CHAPTER XII

REVEALS A CURIOUS PROBLEM

The countenance of Enid Orlebar had changed; her cheeks were deathly white, and her face was sufficient index to a mind overwhelmed with grief and regret.

"I asked you to explain, because I fear that my information may be faulty. Captain Bellairs died – *died suddenly*, did he not?"

"Yes. It was a great blow to my stepfather," the girl said; "and – and by his unfortunate death I lost one of my best friends."

"Tell me exactly how it occurred. I believe the tragic event happened on September the second, did it not?"

"Yes," she replied. "Mother and I had been staying at the White Hart at Salisbury while Sir Hugh had been inspecting some troops. Captain Bellairs had been with us, as usual, but had been sent up to London by my stepfather. That same day I returned to London alone on my way to a visit up in Yorkshire, and arrived at Hill Street about seven o'clock. At a quarter to ten at night I received an urgent note from Captain Bellairs, brought by a messenger, and written in a shaky hand, asking me to call at once at his chambers in Half Moon Street. He explained that he had been taken suddenly ill, and that he wished to see me upon a most important and private matter. He asked me to go to him, as it was most urgent. Mother and I had been to his chambers to tea several times before; therefore, realising the urgency of his message, I found a taxi and went at once to him."

She broke off short, and with difficulty swallowed the lump which arose in her throat.

"Well?" asked Fetherston in a low, sympathetic voice.

"When I arrived," she said, "I - I found him lying dead! He had expired just as I ascended the stairs."

"Then you learned nothing, eh?"

"Nothing," she said in a low voice. "I have ever since wondered what could have been the private matter upon which he so particularly desired to see me. He felt death creeping upon him, or - or else he knew himself to be a doomed man - or he would never have penned me that note."

"The letter in question was not mentioned at the inquest?"

"No. My stepfather urged me to regard the affair as a strict secret. He feared a scandal because I had gone to Harry's rooms."

"You have no idea, then, what was the nature of the communication which the captain wished to make to you?" asked the novelist.

"Not the slightest," replied the girl, yet with some hesitation. "It is all a mystery - a mystery which has ever haunted me - a mystery which haunts me now!"

They had halted, and were standing together beneath a great oak, already partially bare of leaves. He looked into her beautiful face, sweet and full of purity as a child's. Then, in a low, intense voice, he said: "Cannot you be quite frank with me, Enid - cannot you give me more minute details of the sad affair? Captain Bellairs was in his usual health that day when he left you at Salisbury, was he not?"

"Oh, yes. I drove him to the station in our car."

"Have you any idea why your stepfather sent him up to London?"

"Not exactly, except that at breakfast he said to my mother that he must send Bellairs up to London. That was all."

"And at his rooms, whom did you find?"

"Barker, his man," she replied. "The story he told me was a curious one, namely, that his master had arrived from Salisbury at two o'clock, and at half-past two had sent him out upon a message down to Richmond. On his return, a little after five, he found his master absent, but the place smelt strongly of perfume, which seemed to point to the fact that the captain had had a lady visitor."

"He had no actual proof of that?" exclaimed Fetherston, interrupting.

"I think not. He surmised it from the fact that his master disliked scent, even in his toilet soap. Again, upon the table in the hall Barker's quick eye noticed a small white feather; this he showed me, and it was evidently from a feather boa. In the fire-grate a letter had been burnt. These two facts had aroused the manservant's curiosity."

"What time did the captain return?"

"Almost immediately. He changed into his dinner jacket, and went forth again, saying that he intended to dine at the Naval and Military Club, and return to his rooms in time to change and catch the eleven-fifteen train from Waterloo for Salisbury that same night. He even told Barker which suit of clothes to prepare. It seems, however, that he came in about a quarter-past nine, and sent Barker on a message to Waterloo Station. On the man's return he found his master fainting in his armchair. He called Barker to get him a glass of water - his throat seemed on fire, he said. Then, obtaining pen and paper, he wrote that hurried message to me. Barker stated that three minutes after addressing the envelope he fell into a state of coma, the only word he uttered being my name." And she pressed her lips together.

"It is evident, then, that he earnestly desired to speak to you - to tell you something," her companion remarked.

"Yes," she went on quickly. "I found him lying back in his big armchair, quite dead. Barker had feared to leave his side, and summoned the doctor and messenger-boy by telephone. When I entered, however, the doctor had not arrived."

"It was a thousand pities that you were too late. He wished to make some important statement to you, without a doubt."

"I rushed to him at once, but, alas! Was just too late."

"He carried that secret, whatever it was, with him to the grave," Fetherston said reflectively. "I wonder what it could have been?"

"Ah!" sighed the girl, her face yet paler. "I wonder – I constantly wonder."

"The doctors who made the postmortem could not account for the death, I believe. I have read the account of the inquest."

"Ah! Then you know what transpired there," the girl said quickly. "I was in court, but was not called as a witness. There was no reason why I should be asked to make any statement, for Barker, in his evidence, made no mention of the letter which the dead man had sent me. I sat and heard the doctors – both of whom expressed themselves puzzled. The coroner put it to them whether they suspected foul play, but the reply they gave was a distinctly negative one."

"The poor fellow's death was a mystery," her companion said. "I noticed that an open verdict was returned."

"Yes. The most searching inquiry was made, although the true facts regarding it were never made public. Sir Hugh explained one day at the breakfast-table that in addition to the two doctors who made the examination of the body, Professors Dale and Boyd, the analysts of the Home Office, also made extensive experiments, but could detect no symptom of poisoning."

"Where he had dined that night has never been discovered, eh?"

"Never. He certainly did not dine at the club."

"He may have dined with his lady visitor," Fetherston remarked, his eyes fixed upon her.

She hesitated for a moment, as though unwilling to admit that Bellairs should have entertained the unknown lady in secret.

"He may have done so, of course," she said with some reluctance.

"Was there any other fact beside the feather which would lead one to suppose that a lady had visited him?"

"Only the perfume. Barker declared that it was a sweet scent, such as he had never smelt before. The whole place 'reeked with it,' as he put it."

"No one saw the lady call at his chambers?"

"Nobody came forward with any statement," replied the girl. "I myself made every inquiry possible, but, as you know, a woman is much handicapped in such a matter. Barker, who was devoted to his master, spared no effort, but he has discovered nothing."

"For aught we know to the contrary, Captain Bellairs' death may have been due to perfectly natural causes," Fetherston remarked.

"It may have been, but the fact of his mysterious lady visitor, and that he dined at some unknown place on that evening, aroused my suspicions. Yet there was no evidence whatever either of poison or of foul play."

Fetherston raised his eyes and shot a covert glance at her – a glance of distinct suspicion. His keen, calm gaze was upon her, noting the unusual expression upon her countenance, and how her gloved fingers had clenched themselves slightly as she had spoken. Was she telling him all that she knew concerning the extraordinary affair? That was the question which had arisen at that moment within his mind.

He had perused carefully the cold, formal reports which had appeared in the newspapers concerning the "sudden death" of Captain Henry Bellairs, and had read suspicion between the lines, as only one versed in mysteries of crime could read. Were not such mysteries the basis of his profession? He had been first attracted by it as a possible plot for a novel, but, on investigation, had discovered, to his surprise, that Bellairs had been Sir Hugh's trusted secretary and the friend of Enid Orlebar.

The poor fellow had died in a manner both sudden and mysterious, as a good many persons die annually. To the outside world there was no suspicion whatever of foul play.

Yet, being in possession of certain secret knowledge, Fetherston had formed a theory - one that was amazing and startling - a theory which he had, after long deliberation, made up his mind to investigate and prove.

This girl had loved Harry Bellairs before he had met her, and because of it the poor fellow had fallen beneath the hand of a secret assassin.

She stood there in ignorance that he had already seen and closely questioned Barker in London, and that the man had made an admission, an amazing statement - namely, that the subtle Eastern perfume upon Enid Orlebar, when she arrived so hurriedly and excitedly at Half Moon Street, was the same which had greeted his nostrils when he entered his master's chambers on his return from that errand upon which he had been sent.

Enid Orlebar had been in the captain's rooms during his absence!

CHAPTER XIII

THE MYSTERIOUS MR. MALTWOOD

Now Enid Orlebar's story contained several discrepancies.

She had declared that she arrived at Hill Street about seven o'clock on that fateful second of September. That might be true, but might she not have arrived after her secret visit to Half Moon Street?

In suppressing the fact that she had been there at all she had acted with considerable foresight. Naturally, her parents were not desirous of the fact being stated publicly that she had gone alone to a bachelor's rooms, and they had, therefore, assisted her to preserve the secret - known only to Barker and to the doctor. Yet her evidence had been regarded as immaterial, hence she had not been called as witness.

Only Barker had suspected. That unusual perfume about her had puzzled him. Yet how could he make any direct charge against the general's stepdaughter, who had always been most generous to him in the matter of tips? Besides, did not the captain write a note to her with his last dying effort?

What proof was there that the pair had not dined together? Fetherston had already made diligent inquiries at Hill Street, and had discovered from the butler that Miss Enid, on her arrival home from Salisbury, had changed her gown and gone out in a taxi at a quarter to eight. She had dined out - but where was unknown.

It was quite true that she had come in before ten o'clock, and soon afterwards had received a note by boy-messenger.

In view of these facts it appeared quite certain to Fetherston that Enid and Harry Bellairs had taken dinner *tête-à-tête* at some quiet restaurant. She was a merry, high-spirited girl to whom such an adventure would certainly appeal.

After dinner they had parted, and he had driven to his rooms. Then, feeling his strength failing, he had hastily summoned her to his side.

Why?

If he had suspected her of being the author of any foul play he most certainly would not have begged her to come to him in his last moments. No. The enigma grew more and more inscrutable.

And yet there was a motive for poor Bellairs' tragic end – one which, in the light of his own knowledge, seemed only too apparent.

He strolled on beside the fair-faced girl, deep in wonder. Recollections of that devil-may-care cavalry officer who had been such a good friend clouded her brow, and as she walked her eyes were cast upon the ground in silent reflection.

She was wondering whether Walter Fetherston had guessed the truth, that she had loved that man who had met with such an untimely end.

Her companion, on his part, was equally puzzled. That story of Barker's finding a white feather was a curious one. It was true that the man had found a white feather – but he had also learnt that when Enid Orlebar had arrived at Hill Street she had been wearing a white feather boa!

"It is not curious, after all," he said reflectively, "that the police should have dismissed the affair as a death from natural causes. At the inquest no suspicion whatever was aroused. I wonder why Barker, in his evidence, made no mention of that perfume – or of the discovery of the feather?"

And as he uttered those words he fixed his grave eyes upon her, watching her countenance intently.

"Well," she replied, after a moment's hesitation, "if he had it would have proved nothing, would it? If the captain had received a lady visitor in secret that afternoon it might have had no connection with the circumstances of his death six hours later."

"And yet it might," Fetherston remarked. "What more natural than that the lady who visited him clandestinely – for Barker had, no doubt, been sent out of the way on purpose that he should not see her – should have dined with him later?"

The girl moved uneasily, tapping the ground with her stick.

"Then you suspect some woman of having had a hand in his death?" she exclaimed in a changed voice, her eyes again cast upon the ground.

"I do not know sufficient of the details to entertain any distinct suspicion," he replied. "I regard the affair as a mystery, and in mysteries I am always interested."

"You intend to bring the facts into a book," she remarked. "Ah! I see."

"Perhaps – if I obtain a solution of the enigma – for enigma it certainly is."

"You agree with me, then, that poor Harry was the victim of foul play?" she asked in a low, intense voice, eagerly watching his face the while.

"Yes," he answered very slowly, "and, further, that the woman who visited him that afternoon was an accessory. Harry Bellairs was *murdered!*"

Her cheeks blanched and she went pale to the lips. He saw the sudden change in her, and realised what a supreme effort she was making to betray no undue alarm. But the effect of his cold, calm words had been almost electrical. He watched her countenance slowly flushing, but pretended not to notice her confusion. And so he walked on at her side, full of wonderment.

How much did she know? Why, indeed, had Harry Bellairs fallen the victim of a secret assassin?

No trained officer of the Criminal Investigation Department was more ingenious in making secret inquiries, more clever in his subterfuges or in disguising his real objects, than Walter Fetherston. Possessed of ample means, and member of that secret club called "Our Society," which meets at intervals and is the club of criminologists, and pursuing the detection of crime as a pastime, he had on many occasions placed Scotland Yard and the Sûreté in Paris in possession of information which had amazed them and which had earned for him the high esteem of those in office as Ministers of the Interior in Paris, Rome and in London.

The case of Captain Henry Bellairs he had taken up merely because he recognised in it some unusual circumstances, and without sparing effort he had investigated it rapidly and secretly from every standpoint. He had satisfied himself. Certain knowledge that he had was not possessed by any officer at Scotland Yard, and only by reason of that secret knowledge had he been able to arrive at the definite conclusion that there had been a strong motive for the captain's death, and that if he had been secretly poisoned – which seemed to be the case, in spite of the analysts' evidence – then he had been poisoned by the velvet hand of a woman.

Walter Fetherston was ever regretting his inability to put any of the confidential information he acquired into his books.

"If I could only write half the truth of what I know, people would declare it to be fiction," he had often assured intimate friends. And those friends had pondered and wondered to what he referred.

He wrote of crime, weaving those wonderful romances which held breathless his readers in every corner of the globe, and describing criminals and life's undercurrents with such fidelity that even criminals themselves had expressed wonder as to how and whence he obtained his accurate information.

But the public were in ignorance that, in his character of Mr. Maltwood, he pursued a strange profession, one which was fraught with more romance and excitement than any other calling a man could adopt. In comparison with his life that of a detective was really a tame one; while such success had he obtained that in a certain important official circle in London he was held in highest esteem and frequently called into consultation.

Walter Fetherston, the quiet, reticent novelist, was entirely different from the gay, devil-may-care Maltwood, the accomplished linguist, thorough-going cosmopolitan and constant traveller, the easy-going man of means known in society in every European capital.

Because of this his few friends who were aware of his dual personality were puzzled.

At the girl's side he strode on along the road which still led through the wood, the road over which every evening rumbled the old post-diligence on its way through the quaint old town of Etain to the railway at Spincourt. On that very road a battalion of Uhlans had been annihilated almost to a man at the outbreak of the Great War.

Every mètre they trod was historic ground – ground which had been contested against the legions of the Crown Prince's army.

For some time neither spoke. At last Walter asked: "Your stepfather has been up to the fortress with Monsieur Le Pontois, I suppose?"

"Yes, once or twice," was her reply, eager to change the subject. "Of course, to a soldier, fortifications and suchlike things are always of interest."

"I saw them walking up to the fortress together the other day," he remarked with a casual air.

"What?" she asked quickly. "Have you been here before?"

"Once," he laughed. "I came over from Commercy and spent the day in your vicinity in the hope that I might perhaps meet you alone accidentally."

He did not tell her that he had watched her shopping with Madame Le Pontois, or that he had spent several days at a small *auberge* at the tiny village of Marcheville-en-Woevre, only two miles distant.

"I had no idea of that," she replied, her face flushing slightly.

"When do you return to London?" he asked.

"I hardly know. Certainly not before next Thursday, as we have amateur theatricals at General Molon's. I am playing the part of Miss Smith, the English governess, in Darbour's comedy, *Le Pyrée*."

"And then you return to London, eh?"

"I hardly know. Yesterday I had a letter from Mrs. Caldwell saying that she contemplated going to Italy this winter; therefore, perhaps mother will let me go. I wrote to her this morning. The proposal is to spend part of the time in Italy, and then cross from Naples to Egypt. I love Egypt. We were there some winters ago, at the Winter Palace at Luxor."

"Your father and mother will remain at home, I suppose?"

"Mother hates travelling nowadays. She says she had quite sufficient of living abroad in my father's lifetime. We were practically exiled for years, you know. I was born in Lima, and I never saw England till I was eleven. The Diplomatic Service takes one so out of touch with home."

"But Sir Hugh will go abroad this winter, eh?"

"I have not heard him speak of it. I believe he's too busy at the War Office just now. They have some more 'reforms' in progress, I hear," and she smiled.

He was looking straight into the girl's handsome face, his heart torn between love and suspicion.

Those days at Biarritz recurred to him; how he would watch for her and go and meet her down towards Grande Plage, till, by degrees, it had become to both the most natural thing in the world. On those rare evenings when they did not meet the girl was conscious of a little feeling of disappointment which she was too shy to own, even to her own heart.

Walter Fetherston owned it freely enough. In that bright springtime the day was incomplete unless he saw her; and he knew that, even now, every hour was making her grow dearer to him. From that chance meeting at the hotel their friendship had grown, and had ripened into something warmer, dearer - a secret held closely in each heart, but none the less sweet for that.

After leaving Biarritz the man had torn himself from her - why, he hardly knew. Only he felt upon him some fatal fascination, strong and irresistible. It was the first time in his life that he had been what is vulgarly known as "over head and ears in love."

He returned to England, and then, a month later, his investigation of Henry Bellairs' death, for the purpose of obtaining a plot for a new novel he contemplated, revealed to him a staggering and astounding truth.

Even then, in face of that secret knowledge he had gained, he had been powerless, and he had gone up to Monifieth deliberately again to meet her - to be drawn again beneath the spell of those wonderful eyes.

There was love in the man's heart. But sometimes it embittered him. It did at that moment, as they strolled still onward over that carpet of moss and fallen leaves. He had loved her, as he believed her to be a woman with heart and soul too pure to harbour an evil thought. But her story of the death of poor Bellairs, the man who had loved her, had convinced him that his suspicions were, alas, only too well grounded.

CHAPTER XIV

WHAT CONFESSION WOULD MEAN

A silence had fallen between the pair. Again Walter Fetherston glanced at her.

She was an outdoor girl to the tips of her fingers. At shooting parties she went out with the guns, not merely contenting herself, as did the other girls, to motor down with the luncheon for the men. She never got dishevelled or untidy, and her trim tweed skirt and serviceable boots never made her look unwomanly. She was her dainty self out in the country with the men, just as in the pretty drawing-room at Hill Street, while her merry laugh evoked more smiles and witticisms than the more studied attempts at wit of the others.

At that moment she had noticed the change in the man she had so gradually grown to love, and her heart was beating in wild tumult.

He, on his part, was hating himself for so foolishly allowing her to steal into his heart. She had lied to him there, just as she had lied to him at Biarritz. And yet he had been a fool, and had allowed himself to be drawn back to her side.

Why? He asked himself. Why? There was a reason, a strong reason. He loved her, and the reason he was at that moment at her side was to save her, to rescue her from a fate which he knew must sooner or later befall her.

She made some remark, but he only replied mechanically. His countenance had, she saw, changed and become paler. His lips were pressed together, and, taking a cigar from his case, he asked her permission to smoke, and viciously bit off its end. Something had annoyed him. Was it possible that he held any suspicion of the ghastly truth?

The real fact, however, was that he was calmly and deliberately contemplating tearing her from his heart for ever as an object of suspicion and worthless. He, who had never yet fallen beneath a woman's thraldom, resolved not to enter blindly the net she had spread for him. His thoughts were hard and bitter – the thoughts of a man who had loved passionately, but whose idol had suddenly been shattered.

Again she spoke, remarking that it was time she turned back, for already they were at the opposite end of the wood, with a beautiful panorama of valley and winding river spread before them. But he only answered a trifle abruptly, and, acting upon her suggestion, turned and retraced his steps in silence.

At last, as though suddenly rousing himself, he turned to her, and said in an apologetic tone: "I fear, Enid, I've treated you rather – well, rather uncouthly. I apologise. I was thinking of something else – a somewhat serious matter."

"I knew you were," she laughed, affecting to treat the matter lightly. "You scarcely replied to me."

"Forgive me, won't you?" he asked, smiling again in his old way.

"Of course," she said. "But – but is the matter very serious? Does it concern yourself?"

"Yes, Enid, it does," he answered.

And still she walked on, her eyes cast down, much puzzled.

Two woodsmen passed on their way home from work, and raised their caps politely, while Walter acknowledged their salutation in French.

"I shall probably leave here tomorrow," her companion said as they walked back to the high road. "I am not yet certain until I receive my letters tonight."

"You are now going back to your village inn, I suppose," she laughed cheerfully.

"Yes," he said. "My host is an interesting old countryman, and has told me quite a lot about the war. He was wounded when the Germans shelled Verdun. He has told me that he knows Paul Le Pontois, for his son Jean is his servant."

"Why, Mr. Fetherston, you are really ubiquitous," cried the girl in confusion. "Why have you been watching us like this?"

"Merely because I wished to see you, as I've already explained," was his reply. "I wanted to ask you those questions which I have put to you this afternoon."

"About poor Harry?" she remarked in a hoarse, low voice. "But you begged me to reply to you in my own interests - why?"

"Because I wished to know the real truth."

"Well, I've told you the truth," she said with just the slightest tinge of defiance in her voice.

For a moment he did not speak. He had halted; his grave eyes were fixed upon her.

"Have you told me the whole truth - all that you know, Enid?" he asked very quietly a moment later.

"What more should I know?" she protested after a second's hesitation.

"How can I tell?" he asked quickly. "I only ask you to place me in possession of all the facts within your knowledge."

"Why do you ask me this?" she cried. "Is it out of mere idle curiosity? Or is it because - because, knowing that Harry loved me, you wish to cause me pain by recalling those tragic circumstances?"

"Neither," was his quiet answer in a low, sympathetic voice. "I am your friend, Enid. And if you will allow me, I will assist you."

She held her breath. He spoke as though he were aware of the truth –
that she had not told him everything – that she was still concealing
certain important and material facts.

"I – I know you are my friend," she faltered. "I have felt that all
along, ever since our first meeting. But – but forgive me, I beg of you.
The very remembrance of that night of the second of September is, to
me, horrible – horrible."

To him those very words of hers increased his suspicion. Was it any
wonder that she was horrified when she recalled that gruesome episode
of the death of a brave and honest man? Her personal fascination had
overwhelmed Harry Bellairs, just as it had overwhelmed himself. The
devil sends some women into the hearts of upright men to rend and
destroy them.

Upon her cheeks had spread a deadly pallor, while in the centre of
each showed a scarlet spot. Her heart was torn by a thousand emotions,
for the image of that man whom she had seen lying cold and dead in
his room had arisen before her vision, blotting out everything. The
hideous remembrance of that fateful night took possession of her soul.

In silence they walked on for a considerable time. Now and then a
rabbit scuttled from their path into the undergrowth or the alarm-cry of
a bird broke the evening stillness, until at last they came forth into the
wide highway, their faces set towards the autumn sunset.

Suddenly the man spoke.

"Have you heard of the doctor since you left London?" he asked.

She held her breath – only for a single second. But her hesitation was
sufficient to show him that she intended to conceal the truth.

"No," was her reply. "He has not written to me."

Again he was silent. There was a reason – a strong reason – why
Weirmarsh should not write to her, he knew. But he had, by his

question, afforded her an opportunity of telling him the truth – the truth that the mysterious George Weirmarsh was there, in that vicinity. That Enid was aware of that fact was certain to him.

"I wish," she said at last, "I wish you would call at the château and allow me to introduce you to Paul and his wife. They would be charmed to make your acquaintance."

"Thank you," he replied a trifle coldly; "I'd rather not know them – in the present circumstances."

"Why, how strange you are!" the girl exclaimed, looking up into his face, so dark and serious. "I don't see why you should entertain such an aversion to being introduced to Paul. He's quite a dear fellow."

"Perhaps it is a foolish reluctance on my part," he laughed uneasily. "But, somehow, I feel that to remain away from the château is best. Remember, your stepfather and your mother are in ignorance of – well, of the fact that we regard each other as – as more than close friends. For the present it is surely best that I should not visit your relations. Relations are often very prompt to divine the real position of affairs. Parents may be blind," he laughed, "but brothers-in-law never."

"You are always so dreadfully philosophical!" the girl cried, glad that at last that painful topic of conversation had been changed. "Paul Le Pontois wouldn't eat you!"

"I don't suppose any Frenchman is given to cannibalistic diet," he answered, smiling. "But the fact is, I have my reasons for not being introduced to the Le Pontois family just now."

The girl looked at him sharply, surprised at the tone of his response. She tried to divine its meaning. But his countenance still bore that sphinx-like expression which so often caused his friends to entertain vague suspicions.

Few men could read character better than Walter Fetherston. To him the minds of most men and women he met were as an open book. To a marvellous degree had he cultivated his power of reading the inner working of the mind by the expression in the eyes and on the faces of even those hard-headed diplomats and men of business whom, in his second character of Mr. Maltwood, he so frequently met. Few men or women could tell him a deliberate lie without its instant detection. Most shrewd men possess that power to a greater or less degree – a power that can be developed by painstaking application and practice.

Enid asked her companion when they were to meet again.

"At least let me see you before you go from here," she said. "I know what a rapid traveller you always are."

"Yes," he sighed. "I'm often compelled to make quick journeys from one part of the Continent to the other. I am a constant traveller – too constant, perhaps, for I've nowadays grown very world-weary and restless."

"Well," she exclaimed, "if you will not come to the château, where shall we meet?"

"I will write to you," he replied. "At this moment my movements are most uncertain – they depend almost entirely upon the movements of others. At any moment I may be called away. But a letter to Holles Street will always find me, you know."

He seemed unusually serious and strangely preoccupied, she thought. She noticed, too, that he had flung away his half-consumed cigar in impatience, and that he had rubbed his chin with his left hand, a habit of his when puzzled.

At the crossroads where the leafless poplars ran in straight lines towards the village of Fresnes, a big red motor-car passed them at a tearing pace, and in it Enid recognised General Molon.

Fetherston, although an ardent motorist himself, cursed the driver under his breath for bespattering them with mud. Then, with a word of apology to his charming companion, he held her gloved hand for a moment in his.

Their parting was not prolonged. The man's lips were thin and hard, for his resolve was firm.

This girl whom he had grown to love – who was the very sunshine of his strange, adventurous life – was, he had at last realised, unworthy. If he was to live, if the future was to have hope and joy for him, he must tear her out of his life.

Therefore he bade her adieu, refusing to give her any tryst for the morrow.

"It is all so uncertain," he repeated. "You will write to me in London if you do not hear from me, won't you?"

She nodded, but scarce a word, save a murmured farewell, escaped her dry lips.

He was changed, sadly changed, she knew. She turned from him with overflowing heart, stifling her tears, but with a veritable volcano of emotion within her young breast.

He had changed – changed entirely and utterly in that brief hour and a half they had walked together. What had she said? What had she done? She asked herself.

Forward she went blindly with the blood-red light of the glorious sunset full in her hard-set face, the great fortress-crowned hills looming up before her, a barrier between herself and the beyond! They looked grey, dark, mysterious as her own future.

She glanced back, but he had turned upon his heel, and she now saw his retreating figure swinging along the straight, broad highway.

Why had he treated her thus? Was it possible, she reflected, that he had actually become aware of the ghastly truth? Had he divined it?

"If he has," she cried aloud in an agony of soul, "then no wonder – no wonder, indeed, that he has cast me from his life as a criminal – as a woman to be avoided as the plague – that he has said good-bye to me for ever!"

Her lips trembled, and the corners of her pretty mouth hardened.

She turned again to watch the man's disappearing figure.

"I would go back," she cried in despair, "back to him, and beg his forgiveness upon my knees. I love him - love him better than my life! Yet to crave forgiveness would be to confess - to tell all I know - the whole awful truth! And I can't do that - no, never! God help me! I - I - I - can't do that!"

And bursting into a flood of hot tears, she stood rigid, her small hands clenched, still watching him until he disappeared from her sight around the bend of the road.

"No," she murmured in a low, hoarse voice, still speaking to herself, "confession would mean death. Rather than admit the truth I would take my own life. I would kill myself, yes, face death freely and willingly, rather than he - the man I love so well - should learn Sir Hugh's disgraceful secret."

CHAPTER XV

THREE GENTLEMEN FROM PARIS

Gaston Darbour's comedy, Le Pyrée, had been played to a large audience assembled in one of the bigger rooms of the long whitewashed artillery barracks outside Ronvaux, where General Molon had his official residence.

The humorous piece had been applauded to the echo – the audience consisting for the most part of military officers in uniform and their wives and daughters, with a sprinkling of the better-class civilians from the various châteaux in the neighbourhood, together with two or three aristocratic parties from Longuyon, Spincourt, and other places.

The honours of the evening had fallen to the young English girl who had played the amusing part of the demure governess, Miss Smith – pronounced by the others "Mees Smeeth." Enid was passionately fond of dramatic art, and belonged to an amateur club in London. Among those present were the author of the piece himself, a dark young man with smooth hair parted in the centre and wearing an exaggerated black cravat.

When the curtain fell the audience rose to chatter and comment, and were a long time before they dispersed. Paul Le Pontois waited for Enid, Sir Hugh accompanying Blanche and little Ninette home in the hired brougham. As the party had a long distance to go, some twelve kilomètres, General Molon had lent Le Pontois his motor-car, which now stood awaiting him with glaring headlights in the barrack-square.

As the hall emptied Paul glanced around him while awaiting Enid. On the walls the French tricolour was everywhere displayed, the revered *drapeau* under which he had so gallantly and nobly served against the Huns.

He presented a spruce appearance in his smart, well-cut evening coat, with the red button of the Legion d'Honneur in his lapel, and to the ladies who wished him "bonsoir" as they filed out he drew his heels together and bowed gallantly.

Outside, the night was cloudy and overcast. In the long rows of the barrack windows lights shone, and somewhere sounded a bugle, while in the shadows could be heard the measured tramp of sentries, the clank of spurs, or the click of rifles as they saluted their officers passing out.

The whole atmosphere was a military one, for, indeed, the little town of Ronvaux is, even in these peace days, scarcely more than a huge camp.

For a few minutes Le Pontois stood chatting to a group of men at the door. They had invited him to come across to their quarters, but he had explained that he was awaiting mademoiselle. So they raised their eyebrows, smiled mischievously, and bade him "bonsoir."

Soldiers were already stacking up the chairs ready for the clearance of the gymnasium for the morrow. Others were coming to water and sweep out the place. Therefore Le Pontois remained outside in the square, waiting in patience.

He was reflecting. That evening, as he had sat with his wife watching the play, he had been seized by a curious feeling for which he entirely failed to account. Behind him there had sat a man and a woman, French without a doubt, but entire strangers. They must, of course, have known one or other of the officers in order to obtain an admission ticket. Nevertheless, they had spoken to no one, and on the fall of the curtain had entered a brougham in waiting and driven off.

Paul had made no comment. By a sudden chance he had, during the entr'acte, risen and gazed around, when the face of the stranger had caught his eyes – a face which he felt was curiously familiar, yet he could not place it. The middle-aged man was dressed with quiet elegance, clean-shaven and keen-faced, apparently a prosperous civilian, while the lady with him was of about the same age and apparently his wife. She was dressed in a high-necked dress of black lace, and wore in her corsage a large circular ornament of diamonds and emeralds.

Twice had Le Pontois taken furtive glances at the stranger whose lined brow was so extraordinarily familiar. It was the face of a deep thinker, a man who had, perhaps, passed through much trouble. Was it possible, he wondered, that he had seen that striking face in some photograph, or perhaps in some illustrated paper? He had racked his brain through the whole performance, but could not decide in what circumstances they had previously met.

From time to time the stranger had joined with the audience in their hearty laughter, or applauded as vociferously as the others, his companion being equally amused at the quaint sayings of the demure "Mees Smeeth."

And even as he stood in the shadows near the general's car awaiting Enid he was still wondering who the pair might be.

At the fall of the curtain he had made several inquiries of the officers, but nobody could give him any information. They were complete strangers – that was all. Even a search among the cards of invitation had revealed nothing.

So Paul Le Pontois remained mystified.

Enid came at last, flushed with success and apologetic because she had kept him waiting. But he only congratulated her, and assisted her into the car. It was a big open one, therefore she wore a thick motor coat and veil as protection against the chill autumn night.

A moment later the soldier-chauffeur mounted to his seat, and slowly they moved across the great square and out by the gates, where the sentries saluted. Then, turning to the right, they were quickly tearing along the highway in the darkness.

Soon they overtook several closed carriages of the home-going visitors, and, ascending the hill, turned from the main road down into a by-road leading through a wooded valley, which was a short cut to the château.

Part of their way led through the great Forêt d'Amblonville, and though Enid's gay chatter was mostly of the play, the defects in the acting and the several amusing *contretemps* which had occurred behind the scenes, her companion's thoughts were constantly of that stranger whose brow was so deeply lined with care.

They expected to overtake Sir Hugh in the brougham, but so long had Enid been changing her gown that they saw nothing of the others.

Just, however, as they were within a hundred yards or so of the gates which gave entrance to the château, and were slowing down in order to swing into the drive, a man emerged from the darkness, calling upon the driver to stop, and, placing himself before the car, held up his hands.

Next instant the figure of a second individual appeared. Enid uttered a cry of alarm, but the second man, who wore a hard felt hat and dark overcoat, reassured her by saying in French:

"Pray do not distress yourself, mademoiselle. There is no cause for alarm. My friend and I merely wish to speak for a moment with Monsieur Le Pontois before he enters his house. For that reason we have presumed to stop your car."

"But who are you?" demanded Le Pontois angrily. "Who are you that you should hold us up like this?"

"Perhaps, m'sieur, it would be better if you descended and escorted mademoiselle as far as your gates. We wish to speak to you for a moment upon a little matter which is both urgent and private."

"Well, cannot you speak here, now, and let us proceed?"

"Not before mademoiselle," replied the man. "It is a confidential matter."

Paul, much puzzled at the curious demeanour of the strangers, reluctantly handed Enid out, and walked with her as far as his own gate, telling her to assure Blanche that he would return in a few moments, when he had heard what the men wanted.

"Very well," she laughed. "I'll say nothing. You can tell her all when you come in."

The girl passed through the gates and up the gravelled drive to the house, when Le Pontois, turning upon his heel to return to the car, was met by the two men, who, he found, had walked closely behind him.

"You are Paul Le Pontois?" inquired the elder of the pair brusquely.

"Of course! Why do you ask that?"

"Because it is necessary," was his businesslike reply. Then he added: "I regret, m'sieur, that you must consider yourself under arrest by order of his Excellency the Minister of Justice."

"Arrest!" gasped the unhappy man. "Are you mad, messieurs?"

"No," replied the man who had spoken.

"We have merely our duty to perform, and have travelled from Paris to execute it."

"With what offence am I charged?" Le Pontois demanded.

"Of that we have no knowledge. As agents of secret police, we are sent here to convey you for interrogation."

The man under arrest stood dumbfounded.

"But at least you will allow me to say farewell to my wife and child – to make excuse to them for my absence?" he urged.

"I regret that is quite impossible, m'sieur. Our orders are to make the arrest and to afford you no opportunity to communicate with anyone."

"But this is cruel, inhuman! His Excellency never meant that, I am quite sure – especially when I am innocent of any crime, as far as I am aware."

"We can only obey our orders, m'sieur," replied the man in the dark overcoat.

"Then may I not write a line to my wife, just one word of excuse?" he pleaded.

The two police agents consulted.

"Well," replied the elder of the pair, who was the one in authority, "if you wish to scribble a note, here are paper and pencil." And he tore a leaf from his notebook and handed it to the prisoner.

By the light of the head-lamps of the car Paul scribbled a few hurried words to Blanche: "I am detained on important business," he wrote. "I will return tomorrow. My love to you both. – Paul."

The detective read it, folded it carefully, and handed it to his assistant, telling him to go up to the château and deliver it at the servants' entrance.

When he had gone the detective, turning to the chauffeur, said: "I shall require you to take us to Verdun."

"This is not my car, m'sieur," replied Paul. "It belongs to General Molon."

"That does not matter. I will telephone to him an explanation as soon as we arrive in Verdun. We may as well enter the car as stand here."

Paul Le Pontois was about to protest, but what could he say? The Minister in Paris had apparently committed some grave error in thus ordering his arrest. No doubt there would be confusion, apologies and laughter. So, with a light heart at the knowledge that he had committed no offence, he got into the car, and allowed the polite police agent to seat himself beside him.

The only chagrin he felt was that the chauffeur had overheard all the conversation. And to him he said: "Remember, Gallet, of this affair you know nothing."

"I understand perfectly, m'sieur," was the wondering soldier's reply.

Then they sat in silence in the darkness until the hurrying police agent returned, after which the car sped straight past the château on the high road which led through the deep valley on to the fortress town of Verdun.

As they passed the château Paul Le Pontois caught a glimpse of its lighted windows and sat wondering what Blanche would imagine. He pictured the pleasant supper party and the surprise that would be expressed at his absence.

How amusing! What incongruity! He was under arrest!

The car rushed on beneath the precipitous hill crowned by the great fortress of Haudiomont, through the narrow gorge – the road to Paris.

All three men, seated abreast, were silent until, at last, the elder of the two police agents bent and glanced at the clock on the dashboard, visible by the tiny glow-lamp.

"Half past twelve," he remarked. "The express leaves Verdun at two twenty-eight."

"For where?" asked Paul.

"For Paris."

"Paris!" he cried. "Are you taking me to Paris?"

"Those are our orders," was the detective's quiet response.

CHAPTER XVI

THE ORDERS OF HIS EXCELLENCY

Again Paul sat back without a word. Well, he would hear the extraordinary charge against him, whatever it might be. And, without speaking, they travelled on and on, until they at last entered the Porte St. Paul at Verdun, passed up the Avenue de la Gare, skirting the Palais de Justice into the station yard.

As Paul descended they were met by a third stranger who strolled forward - a man in a heavy travelling coat and a soft Homburg hat.

It was the man who had sat behind him earlier in the evening - the man with the deep lines upon his care-worn brow, who had laughed so heartily - and who a moment later introduced himself as Jules Pierrepont, special commissaire of the Paris Sûreté.

"We have met before?" remarked Paul abruptly.

"Yes, Monsieur Le Pontois," replied the man with a grim smile. "On several occasions lately. It has been my duty to keep observation upon your movements - acting upon orders from Monsieur the Prefect of Police."

And together they entered the dark, deserted station to await the night express for Paris.

Suddenly Paul turned back, saying to the chauffeur in a low, hard voice: "Gallet, tomorrow go and tell madame my wife that I am unexpectedly called to the capital. Tell her - tell her that I will write to her. But, at all hazards, do not let her know the truth that I am under arrest," he added hoarsely.

"That is understood, monsieur," replied the man, saluting. "Neither madame nor anyone else shall know why you have left for Paris."

"I rely upon you," were Paul's parting words, and, turning upon his heel, he accompanied the three men who were in waiting.

Half an hour later he sat in a second-class compartment of the Paris *rapide* with the three keen-eyed men who had so swiftly effected his arrest.

It was apparent to him now that the reason he had recognised Pierrepont was because that man had maintained vigilant, yet unobtrusive, observation upon him during several of the preceding days, keeping near him in all sorts of ingenious guises and making inquiries concerning him – inquiries instituted for some unexplained cause by the Paris police.

Bitterly he smiled to himself as he gazed upon the faces of his three companions, hard and deep-shadowed beneath the uncertain light. Presently he made some inquiry of Jules Pierrepont, who had now assumed commandership of the party, as to the reason of his arrest.

"I regret, Monsieur Le Pontois," replied the quiet, affable man, "his Excellency does not give us reasons. We obey orders – that is all."

"But surely there is still, even after the war, justice in France!" cried Paul in dismay. "There must be some good reason. One cannot be thus arrested as a criminal without some charge against him – in my case a false one!"

All three men had heard prisoners declare their innocence many times before, therefore they merely nodded assent – it was their usual habit.

"There is, of course, some charge," remarked Pierrepont. "But no doubt monsieur has a perfect answer to it."

"When I know what it is," replied Paul between his teeth, "then I shall meet it bravely, and demand compensation for this outrageous arrest!"

He held his breath, for, with a sinking heart, he realised for the first time the very fact of a serious allegation being made against him by some enemy. If mud is thrown some of it always sticks. What had all his enthusiasm in life profited him? Nothing. He bit his lip when he reflected.

"You have some idea of what is alleged against me, messieurs," the unhappy man exclaimed presently, as the roaring train emerged from a long tunnel. "I see it in your faces. Indeed, you would not have taken the precaution, which you did at the moment of my arrest, of searching me to find firearms. You suspected that I might make an attempt to take my life."

"Merely our habit," replied Pierrepont with a slight smile.

"The charge is a grave one – will you not admit that?"

"Probably it is – or we should not all three have been sent to bring you to Paris," remarked one of the trio.

"You have had access to my *dossier* – I feel sure you have, monsieur," Paul said, addressing Pierrepont.

"Ah! You are in error. Monsieur le Ministre does not afford me that privilege. I am but the servant of the Sûreté, and no one regrets more than myself the painful duty I have been compelled to perform tonight. I assure you, Monsieur Le Pontois, that I entertain much regret that I have been compelled to drag you away from your home and family thus, to Paris."

"No apology is needed, mon ami," Paul exclaimed quickly, well aware that the detective was merely obeying instructions. "I understand your position perfectly." Then, glancing round at his companions, he added: "You may sleep in peace, messieurs. I give you my word of honour that I will not attempt to escape. Why, indeed, should I? I have committed no wrong!"

One of the men had pulled out a well-worn notebook and was with difficulty writing down the prisoner's words – to be put in evidence against him. Le Pontois realised that; therefore his mouth closed with a snap, and, leaning back in the centre of the carriage, he closed his eyes, not to sleep, but to think.

Before leaving Verdun he had seen Pierrepont enter the telegraph bureau – to dispatch a message to the Sûreté, without a doubt. They already knew in Paris that he was under arrest, but at his home they were, happily, still in ignorance. Poor Blanche was asleep, no doubt, by that time, he thought, calm in the belief that he had been delayed and would be home in the early hours.

The fact that he was actually under arrest he regarded with more humour than seriousness, feeling that in the morning explanations would be made and the blunder rectified.

No more honourable or upright man was there in France than Paul Le Pontois, and this order from the Sûreté had held him utterly speechless and astounded. So he sat there hour after hour as the *rapide* roared westward, until it halted at the great echoing station of Châlons, where all four entered the buffet and hastily swallowed their café-au-lait.

Afterwards they resumed their seats, and the train, with its two long, dusty *wagons-lit*, moved onward again, with Paris for its goal.

The prisoner said little. He sat calmly reflecting, wondering and wondering what possible charge could be made against him. He had enemies, as every man had, he knew, but he was not aware of anyone who could make an allegation of a character sufficiently grave to warrant his arrest.

Why had it been forbidden that he should wish Blanche farewell? There was some reason for that! He inquired of Pierrepont, who had treated him with such consideration and even respect, but the agent of secret police only replied that in making an arrest of that character they made it a rule never to allow a prisoner to communicate with his family.

"There are several reasons for it," he explained. "One is that very often the prisoner will make a statement to his wife which he will afterwards greatly regret. Again, prisoners have been known to whisper to their wives secret instructions, to order the destruction of papers before we can make a domiciliary visit, or —"

"But you surely will not make a domiciliary visit to my house?" cried Paul, interrupting.

The men exchanged glances.

"At present we cannot tell," Pierrepont replied. "It depends upon what instructions we receive."

"Do you usually make searches?" asked the prisoner, with visions of his own home being desecrated and ransacked.

"Yes, we generally do," the commissaire of police admitted. "As I have explained, it is for that reason we do not allow a prisoner's wife to know that he is under arrest."

"But such an action is abominable!" cried Le Pontois angrily. "That my house should be turned upside down and searched as though I were a common thief, a forger, or a coiner is beyond toleration. I shall demand full inquiry. My friend Carlier shall put an interpellation in the Chamber!"

"Monsieur le Ministre acts upon his own discretion," the detective replied coldly.

"And by so doing sometimes ruins the prospects and the lives of some of our best men," blurted forth the angry prisoner. It was upon the tip of his tongue to say much more in condemnation, but the sight of the man with the notebook caused him to hesitate.

Every word he uttered now would, he knew, be turned against him.

He was under arrest – for some crime that he had not committed.

The other passengers by that night express, who included a party of English tourists, little dreamed as they passed up and down the corridor that the smart, good-looking man who wore the button of the Legion d'Honneur, and who sat there with the three quiet, respectable-looking men, was being conveyed to the capital under escort – a man who, by the law of France, was already condemned, was guilty until he could prove his own innocence!

In the cold grey of dawn they descended at last at the great bare Gare de l'Est in Paris. Paul felt tired, cramped and unshaven, but of necessity entered a taxi called by one of his companions, and, accompanied by Pierrepont and the elder of his assistants, was driven along through the cheerless, deserted streets to the Sûreté.

As he entered the side door of the ponderous building the police officer on duty saluted his escort.

His progress across France had been swift and secret.

What, he wondered, did the future hold in store for him?

His lip curled into a smile when they ushered him into a bare room on the first floor. Two police officers were placed outside the door, while two stood within.

Then, turning to the window, which looked out upon the bare trees of the Place below, he laughed aloud and made some humorous remark which caused the men to smile.

But, alas, he knew not the truth. Little did he dream of the amazing allegation that was to be made against him! – little did he dream how completely the enemies of his father-in-law, the general, had triumphed!

CHAPTER XVII

WALTER GIVES WARNING

The morning dawned bright and sunny – a perfect autumn morning – at the pretty Château of Lérouville.

The message which Blanche had received after returning had not caused her much consternation. She supposed that Paul had been suddenly called away on business. So she had eaten her supper with her father and Enid and retired to rest.

When, however, they sat at breakfast – served in the English style – Sir Hugh opened a letter which lay upon his plate, and at once announced his intention of returning to London.

"I have to see Hughes, my solicitor, over Aunt Mary's affairs," he explained suddenly to Blanche. "That executorship is always an infernal nuisance."

"But surely you can remain a day or two longer, Dad?" exclaimed Madame Le Pontois. "The weather is delightful just now, and I hear it is too dreadful for words in England."

"I, too, have to be back to prepare for going away with Mrs. Caldwell," Enid remarked.

"But surely these solicitors will wait? There is no great urgency – there can't be! The old lady died ten years ago," Blanche exclaimed as she poured out coffee.

"My dear, I'm extremely sorry," said her father quietly, "but I must go – it is imperative."

"Not today?"

"I ought to go today," he sighed. "Indeed, I really must - by the *rapide* I usually take. Perhaps I shall alter my route this time, and go from Conflans to Metz, and home by Liège and Brussels. It is about as quick, and one gets a *wagon-lit* from Metz. I looked up the train the other day, and find it leaves Conflans at a little after six."

"Surely you will remain and say au revoir to Paul? He'll be so disappointed!" she cried in dismay.

"My dear, you will make excuses for us. I must really go, and so must Enid. She had a letter from Mrs. Caldwell urging her to get back, as she wants to start abroad for the winter. The bad weather in England is affecting her, it seems."

And so, with much regret expressed by little Ninette and her mother, Sir Hugh Elcombe and his stepdaughter went to their rooms to see about their packing.

Both were puzzled. The sudden appearance of those strange men out of the darkness had frightened Enid, but she had said nothing. Perhaps it was upon some private matter that Paul had been summoned. Therefore she had preserved silence, believing with Blanche that at any moment he might return.

Back in his room, Sir Hugh closed the door, and, standing in the sunshine by the window, gazed across the wide valley towards the blue mists beyond, deep in reflection.

"This curious absence of Paul's forebodes evil," he murmured to himself.

He had slept little that night, being filled with strange apprehensions. Though he had closely questioned Enid, she would not say what had actually happened. Her explanation was merely that Paul had been called away by a man who had met him outside.

The old man sighed, biting his lip. He cursed himself for his dastardly work, even though he had been compelled by Weirmarsh to execute it on pain of exposure and consequent ruin.

Against his will, against his better nature, he had been forced to meet the mysterious doctor of Pimlico in secret on that quiet, wooded by-road between Marcheville and Saint-Hilaire, four kilomètres from the château, and there discuss with him the suggested affair of which they had spoken in London.

The two men had met at sundown.

"You seem to fear exposure!" laughed the man who provided Sir Hugh with his comfortable income. "Don't be foolish - there is no danger. Return to England with Enid as soon as you possibly can without arousing suspicion, and I will call and see you at Hill Street. I want to have a very serious chat with you."

Elcombe's grey, weather-worn face grew hard and determined.

"Why are you here, Weirmarsh?" he demanded. "I have helped you and your infernal friends in the past, but please do not count upon my assistance in the future. Remember that from today our friendship is entirely at an end."

"As you wish, of course, my dear Sir Hugh," replied the other, with a nonchalant air. "But if I were you I would not be in too great a hurry to make such a declaration. You may require a friend in the near future - a friend like myself."

"Never, I hope - never!" snapped the old general.

"Very well," replied the doctor, who, with a shrug of his shoulders, wished his friend a cold adieu and, turning, strode away.

As Sir Hugh stood alone by the window that morning he recalled every incident of that hateful interview, every word that had fallen from the lips of the man who seemed to be as ingenious and resourceful as Satan himself.

His anxiety regarding Paul's sudden absence had caused him to invent an excuse for his own hurried departure. He was not prepared to remain there and witness his dear daughter's grief and humiliation, so he deemed it wiser to get away in safety to England, for he no longer trusted Weirmarsh. Suppose the doctor revealed the actual truth by means of some anonymous communication?

As he stood staring blankly across the valley he heard the hum of an approaching motor-car, and saw that it was General Molon's, being driven by Gallet, the soldier chauffeur.

There was no passenger, but the car entered the iron gates and pulled up before the door.

A few minutes later Blanche ran up the stairs and, bursting into her father's room, cried: "Paul has been called suddenly to Paris, Dad! He told Gallet to come this morning and tell me. How strange that he did not come in to get even a valise!"

"Yes, dear," said her father. "Gallet is downstairs, isn't he? I'll speak to him. The mystery of Paul's absence increases!"

"It does. I – I can't get rid of a curious feeling of apprehension that something has happened. What was there to prevent him from coming in to wish me good-bye when he was actually at the gate?"

Sir Hugh went below and questioned the chauffeur.

The story told by the man Gallet was that Le Pontois had been met by two gentlemen and given a message that he was required urgently in Paris, and they had driven at once over to Verdun, where they had just caught the train.

"Did Monsieur Le Pontois leave any other message for madame?" asked Sir Hugh in French.

"No, m'sieur."

The general endeavoured by dint of persuasion to learn something more, but the man was true to his promise, and would make no further statement. Indeed, earlier that morning he had been closely questioned

117

by the commandant, but had been equally reticent. Le Pontois was a favourite in the neighbourhood, and no man would dare to lift his voice against him.

Sir Hugh returned to his room and commenced packing his suitcases, more than ever convinced that suspicion had been aroused. Jean came to offer to assist, but he declared that he liked to pack himself, and this occupied him the greater part of the morning.

Enid was also busy with her dresses, assisted by Blanche's Provençal maid, Louise. About eleven o'clock, however, Jean tapped at her door and said: "A peasant from Allamont, across the valley, has brought a letter, mademoiselle. He says an English gentleman gave it to him to deliver to you personally. He is downstairs."

In surprise the girl hurriedly descended to the servants' entrance, where she found a sturdy, old, grey-bearded peasant, bearing a long, stout stick. He raised his frayed cap politely and asked whether she were Mademoiselle Orlebar.

Then, when she had replied in the affirmative, he drew from the breast of his blouse a crumpled letter, saying: "The Englishman who has been staying at the Lion d'Or at Allamont gave this to me at dawn today. I was to give it only into mademoiselle's hands. There is no reply."

Enid tore open the letter eagerly and found the following words, written hurriedly in pencil in Walter Fetherston's well-known scrawling hand – for a novelist's handwriting is never of the best:

"Make excuse and induce your father to leave Conflans-Jarny at once for Metz, travelling by Belgium for London. Accompany him. A serious *contretemps* has occurred which will affect you both if you do not leave immediately on receipt of this. Heed this, I beg of you. And remember, I am still your friend.

"Walter."

For a moment she stood puzzled. "Did the Englishman say there was no reply?" she asked.

"Yes, mademoiselle. He left the Lion d'Or just before eight, and drove into Conflans with his luggage. The innkeeper told me that he is returning suddenly to England. He received several telegrams in the night, it appears."

"You know him, then?"

"Oh yes, mademoiselle. He came there to fish in the Longeau, and I have been with him on several occasions."

Enid took a piece of "cent sous" from her purse and gave it to the old man, then she returned to her room and, sending Louise below for something, burned Walter's letter in the grate.

Afterwards she went to her stepfather and suggested that perhaps they might leave Conflans earlier than he had resolved.

"I hear there is a train at three-five. If we went by that," she said, "we could cross from Ostend instead of by Antwerp, and thus be in London a day earlier."

"Are you so anxious to get away from here, Enid?" he asked, looking straight into her face.

"Well, yes. Mother, in her letter yesterday, urged me to come home, as she does not wish me to travel out alone to join Mrs. Caldwell. She's afraid she will leave London without me if I don't get home at once. Besides, I've got a lot of shopping to do before I can start. Do let us get away by the earlier train. It will be so much better," she urged.

As Sir Hugh never denied Enid anything, he acquiesced. Packing was speedily concluded, and, much to the regret of Blanche, the pair left in a fly for which they had telephoned to Conflans-Jarny.

The train by which they travelled ran through the beautiful valley of Manvaux, past the great forts of Plappeville and St. Quentin, and across the Moselle to Metz, and so into German territory.

Whatever might happen, Sir Hugh reflected, at least he was now safe from arrest. While Enid, on her part, sat back in the corner of the first-class compartment gazing out of the window, still mystified by that strange warning from the man who only a few days previously had so curiously turned and abandoned her.

CHAPTER XVIII

THE ACCUSERS

At the same hour when Enid and Sir Hugh were passing Amanvilliers, once the scene of terrible atrocities by the Huns, Paul Le Pontois, between two agents of police, was ushered into the private cabinet where, at the great writing-table near the window, sat a short man with bristling hair and snow-white moustache, Monsieur Henri Bézard, chief of the Sûreté Générale.

A keen-faced, black-eyed man of dapper appearance, wearing the coveted button of the Légion d'Honneur in his black frock-coat, he looked up sharply at the man brought into his presence, wished him a curt "bon jour," and motioned him to a seat at the opposite side of the big table, in such a position that the grey light from the long window fell directly upon his countenance.

With him, standing about the big, handsome room with its green-baize doors and huge oil paintings on the walls, were four elderly men, strangers to Paul.

The severe atmosphere of that sombre apartment, wherein sat the chief of the police of the Republic, was depressing. Those present moved noiselessly over the thick Turkey carpet, while the double windows excluded every sound from the busy boulevard below.

"Your name," exclaimed the great Bézard sharply, at last raising his eyes from a file of papers before him - "your name is Paul Robert Le Pontois, son of Paul Le Pontois, rentier of Severac, Department of

121

Aveyron. During the war you were captain in the 114th Regiment of Artillery, and you now reside with your wife and daughter at the Château of Lérouville. Are those details correct?"

"Perfectly, m'sieur," replied the man seated with the two police agents standing behind him. He wore his black evening trousers and a brown tweed jacket which one of the detectives had lent him.

"You have been placed under arrest by order of the Ministry," replied Bézard, speaking in his quick, impetuous way.

"I am aware of that, m'sieur," was Paul's reply, "but I am in ignorance of the charge against me."

"Well," exclaimed Bézard very gravely, again referring to the formidable *dossier* before him, "the charge brought against you is most serious. It is astounding and disgraceful. Listen, and I will read it. Afterwards we will hear what explanation you have to offer. We are assembled for that purpose."

The four other men had taken chairs near by, while Pierrepont was standing at some distance away, with his back to the wood fire.

For a second Bézard paused, then, rubbing his gold pince-nez and adjusting them, he read in a cold, hard voice the following:

"The charge alleged against you, Paul Robert Le Pontois, is that upon four separate occasions you have placed in circulation forged Bank of England and Treasury notes of England to the extent of nearly a million francs."

"It's a lie!" cried Paul, jumping to his feet, his face aflame. "Before God, I swear it is a lie!"

"Calm yourself and listen," commanded the great chief of the Sûreté Générale sharply. "Be seated."

The prisoner sank back into his chair again. His head was reeling. Who could possibly have made such unfounded charges against him? He could scarcely believe his ears.

122

Then the hard-faced, white-headed old director, who held supreme command of the police of the Republic, glanced at him shrewdly, and, continuing, said: "It is alleged that you, Paul Le Pontois, on the fourteenth day of January, and again on the sixteenth of May, met in Commercy a certain Englishman, and handed to him a bundle of English notes since proved to be forgeries."

"I am not acquainted with any English forger," protested Paul.

"Do not interrupt, m'sieur!" snapped the director. "You will, later on, be afforded full opportunity to make any statement or explanation you may wish. First listen to these grave charges against you." After a further pause, he added: "The third occasion, it is alleged, was on April the eighth last, when it seems you drove at early morning over to Thillot-sous-les-Côtes and there met a stranger who was afterwards identified as an American who is wanted for banknote forgeries."

"And the fourth?" asked Paul hoarsely. This string of allegations utterly staggered him.

"The fourth occasion was quite recently," Bézard said, still speaking in that same cold tone. "On that occasion you made certain calculations to ascertain how much were your profits by dealing with these forgers whom Scotland Yard are so anxious to arrest. You wrote all the sums down, knowing your expenditure and profits. The latter were very considerable."

"And by whom is it alleged that I am a dealer in base money, pray?"

"It is not necessary for us to disclose the name of our informant," was the stiff rejoinder.

"But surely I am not to be thus denounced by an anonymous enemy?" he cried. "This is not the justice which every Frenchman claims as his birthright!"

"You have demanded to know the charges laid against you, and I have detailed them," replied the chief of the Sûreté, regarding the prisoner closely through his gold pince-nez.

"They are false - every word of them," promptly returned Le Pontois. "I have no acquaintance with any banknote forger. If I had, he would quickly find himself under arrest."

The four men seated in his vicinity smiled grimly. They had expected the prisoner to declare his innocence.

"I may tell you that the information here" - and Bézard tapped the *dossier* before him - "is from a source in which we have the most complete and implicit confidence. For the past few months there have been suspicions that forged English notes have been put into circulation in France. Therefore I ordered a vigilant watch to be maintained. Monsieur Pierrepont, here, has been in command of a squadron of confidential agents."

"And they have watched me, and, I suppose, have manufactured evidence against me! It is only what may be expected of men paid to spy upon us. If I am a forger or a friend of forgers, as you allege me to be, then I am unworthy to have served in the uniform of France. But I tell you that the allegations you have just read are lies - lies, every word of them." And Le Pontois' pale cheeks flushed crimson with anger.

"Le Pontois," remarked a tall, thin, elderly commissaire who was present, "it is for you to prove your innocence. The information laid before us is derived from those who have daily watched your movements and reported them. If you can prove to us that it is false, then your innocence may be established."

"But I am innocent!" he protested, "therefore I have no fear what charges may be laid against me. They cannot be substantiated. The whole string of allegations is utterly ridiculous!"

"Eh bien! Then let us commence with the first," exclaimed Bézard, again referring to the file of secret reports before him. "On Wednesday, the fourteenth day of January, you went to Commercy, where, at the

Café de la Cloche, you met a certain Belgian who passed under the name of Laloux."

"I recollect!" cried Le Pontois quickly. "I sold him a horse. He was a dealer."

"A dealer in forged notes," remarked one of the officials, with a faint smile.

"Was he a forger, then?" asked Le Pontois in entire surprise.

"Yes. He has entered France several times in the guise of a horsedealer," Pierrepont interrupted.

"But I only bought a horse of him," declared the prisoner vehemently.

"And you paid for it in English notes, apologising that you had no other money. He took them, for he passed them in Belgium into an English bank in Brussels. They were forged!"

"Again, on the sixteenth of May, you met the man Laloux at the same place," said Bézard.

"He had a mare to sell – I tried to buy it for my wife to drive, but he wanted too much."

"You remained the night at the Hôtel de Paris, and saw him again at nine o'clock next morning."

"True. I hoped to strike a bargain with him in the morning, but we could not come to terms."

"Regarding the forged English notes you were prepared to sell, eh?" snapped Bézard, with a look of disbelief.

"I had nothing to sell!" protested Le Pontois, drawing himself up. "Those who have spied upon me have told untruths."

"But the individual, Laloux, was watched. One of our agents followed him to Brussels, where he went next day to the English bank in the Montagne de la Cour."

"Not with forged notes from me. My dealings with him were in every way honest business transactions."

"You mean that you received money from him, eh?"

"I do not deny that. I sold him a horse on the first occasion. He paid me seven hundred francs for it, and I afterwards purchased one from him."

"So you do not deny that you received money from that man?"

"Why should I? I sold him a horse, and he paid me for it."

"Very well," said Bézard, with some hesitation. "Let us pass to the eighth of April. At six o'clock that morning you drove to Thillot-sous-les-Côtes, where you met a stranger at the entrance to the village, and walked with him, and held a long and earnest conversation."

Paul was silent for a moment. The incident recalled was one that he would fain have forgotten, one the truth of which he intended at all hazards to conceal.

"I admit that I went to Thillot in secret," he answered in a changed voice.

"Ah! Then you do not deny that you were attracted by the promises of substantial payment for certain forged English notes which you could furnish, eh?" grunted Bézard in satisfaction.

"I admit going to Thillot, but I deny your allegation," cried Paul in quick protest.

"Then perhaps you will tell us the reason you took that early drive?" asked a commissaire, with a short, hard laugh of disbelief.

The prisoner hesitated. It was a purely personal matter, one which concerned himself alone.

"I regret, messieurs," was his slow reply, "I regret that I am unable – indeed, I am not permitted to answer that question."

"Pray why?" inquired Bézard.

"Well – because it concerns a woman's honour," was the low, hoarse reply, "the honour of the wife of a certain officer."

At those words of his the men interrogating him laughed in derision, declaring it to be a very elegant excuse.

"It is no excuse!" he cried fiercely, again rising from his chair. "When I have obtained permission to speak, messieurs, I will tell you the truth. Until then I shall remain silent."

"Eh, bien!" snapped Bézard. "And so we will pass to the next and final charge – that you prepared a statement in order to satisfy yourself regarding the profits of your dealings in these spurious notes."

"I have no knowledge of such a thing!" Paul replied instantly.

"And yet for several weeks past a mysterious friend of yours has been seen in the neighbourhood of your château. He has been staying in Commercy and in Longuyon. I gave orders for his arrest, but, with his usual cleverness, he escaped from Commercy."

"I prepared no statement."

"H'm!" grunted Bézard, looking straight into his flushed face. "You are quite certain of that?"

"I swear I did not."

"Then perhaps you will deny that this is in your hand?" the director asked slowly, with a grin, as he fixed his eyes upon Paul and handed him a sheet of his own note-paper bearing the address of the château embossed in green.

Paul took it in his trembling fingers, and as he did so his countenance fell.

It was the rough account of his investments and profits he remembered making for his father-in-law. He had cast it unheeded into the waste-paper basket, whence it had, no doubt, been recovered by those who had spied upon him and placed with the reports as evidence against him.

"You admit making that calculation?" asked Bézard severely. "Those figures are, I believe, in your handwriting?"

"Yes; but I have had nothing to do with any forgers of banknotes," declared the unhappy man, reseating himself.

"Ah! Then you admit making the calculation? That in itself is sufficient for the present. However, cannot you give us some explanation of that secret visit of yours to Thillot? Remember, you have to prove your innocence!"

"I – I cannot – not, at least, at present," faltered the prisoner.

"You refuse?"

"Yes, m'sieur, I flatly refuse," was the hoarse reply. "As I have told you, that visit concerned the honour of a woman."

The men again exchanged glances of disbelief, while the victim of those dastardly allegations sat breathless, amazed at the astounding manner in which his most innocent actions had been misconstrued into incriminating evidence.

He was under arrest as one who had placed forged English banknotes in circulation in France!

CHAPTER XIX

IN WHICH A TRUTH IS HIDDEN

When Walter Fetherston entered the tasteful drawing-room at Hill Street four days later he found Enid alone, seated by the fire.

The dull London light of the autumn afternoon was scarcely sufficient for him to distinguish every object in the apartment, but as he advanced she rose and stood silhouetted against the firelight, a slight, graceful figure, with hand outstretched.

"Both mother and Sir Hugh are out – gone to a matinée at the Garrick," she exclaimed. "I'm so glad you've come in," and she placed a chair for him.

"I have heard that you are leaving for Egypt tomorrow," he said, "and I wished to have a chat with you."

"We go to Italy first, and to Egypt after Christmas," she replied. "Mother has promised to join us in Luxor at the end of January."

"If I were you, Enid," he replied gravely, bending towards her, "I would make some excuse and remain in England."

"Why?" she asked, her eyes opening widely. "I don't understand!"

"I regret that I am unable to speak more plainly," he said. "I warned you to leave France, and I was glad that you and Sir Hugh heeded my warning. Otherwise – well, perhaps an unpleasant incident would have resulted."

"You always speak in enigmas nowadays," said the girl, again standing near the fireplace, dainty in her dark skirt and cream silk jumper. "Why did you send me that extraordinary note?"

"In your own interests," was his vague reply. "I became aware that your further presence in the house of Monsieur Le Pontois was – well – undesirable – that's all."

"I really think you entertain some antagonism against Paul," she declared, "yet he's such a good fellow."

The novelist's eyes sparkled through his pince-nez as he replied: "He's very good-looking, I admit, and, no doubt, a perfect cavalier."

"You suspect me of flirtations with him, of course," she pouted. "Well, you're not the first man who has chaffed me about that."

"No, no," he laughed. "I'm in no way jealous, I assure you. I merely told you that your departure from the château would be for the best."

He did not tell her that within an hour of their leaving French territory an official telegram had been received from Paris by the local commissaire of police with orders to detain them both, nor that just before dark an insignificant-looking man in black had called at the château and been informed by Jean that the English general and his stepdaughter had already departed.

The whole of that night the wires between the sous-prefecture at Briey and Paris had been at work, and many curious official messages had been exchanged. Truly, the pair had had a providential escape.

Sir Hugh was, of course, in entire ignorance of the dastardly action taken by the Pimlico doctor.

Without duly counting the cost, he had declared at his last interview with Weirmarsh that their criminal partnership was now at an end. And the doctor had taken him at his word.

Had not the doctor in London told his assistant, Heureux, that Sir Hugh's sphere of usefulness was at an end, and that, in all probability, a *contretemps* would occur – one which would in future save to "the syndicate" the sum of five thousand pounds per annum?

Truth to tell, Bézard, director of the Sûreté, had telegraphed orders for the arrest of Sir Hugh and his daughter. But, thanks to the shrewdness of Fetherston, who had lingered in the vicinity to afford them protection if necessary, they had succeeded in escaping only a single hour before the message reached its destination.

Neither of them knew of this, and the novelist intended that they should remain in ignorance – just as they were still in ignorance of the reason of Paul's visit to Paris and of his detention there.

If they were aware of the reason of his warning, then they would most certainly question him as to the manner in which he was able to gain knowledge of the betrayal by Weirmarsh. He had no desire to be questioned upon such matters. The motives of his action – always swift, full of shrewd foresight, and often in disregard of his own personal safety – were known alone to himself and to Scotland Yard.

If the truth were told, he had not been alone in Eastern France. At the little old-world Croix-Blanche at Briey a stout, middle-aged, ruddy-faced English tourist had had his headquarters; while, again, at the unpretending Cloche d'Or in the Place St. Paul at Verdun another Englishman, a young, active, clean-shaven man, had been moving about the country in constant communication with "Mr. Maltwood." Wherever the doctor from Pimlico and his assistant, Heureux, had gone, there also went one or other of those two sharp-eyed but unobtrusive Englishmen. Every action of the doctor had been noted, and information of it conveyed to the quiet-mannered man in pince-nez.

"Really, Walter, you are quite as mysterious as your books," Enid was declaring, with a laugh. "I do wish you would satisfy my curiosity and tell me why you urged me to leave France so suddenly."

"I had reasons – strong reasons which you may, perhaps, some day know," was his response. "I am only glad that you thought fit to take the advice I offered. This afternoon I have called to give you further advice – namely, to remain in England, at least for the present."

"But I can't. My friend Jane Caldwell has been waiting a whole fortnight for me, suffering from asthma in these abominable fogs."

"You can make some excuse. I assure you that to remain in London will be for the best," he said, while she switched on the shaded electric lights, which shed a soft glow over the handsome room – that apartment, the costly furniture of which had been purchased out of the money secretly supplied by Weirmarsh.

"But I can't see why I should remain," she protested, facing him again. He noted how strikingly handsome she was, her dimpled cheeks delicately moulded and her pretty chin slightly protruding, which gave a delightful piquancy to her features.

"I wish I could explain further. I can't at present!"

"You are, as I have already said, so amazingly mysterious – so full of secrets always!"

The man sighed, his brows knit slightly.

"Yes," he said, "I am full of secrets – strange, astounding secrets they are – secrets which some time, if divulged, would mean terrible complications, ruin to those who are believed to be honest and upright."

The girl stood for a few seconds in silence.

She had heard strange rumours regarding the man seated there before her. Some had hinted that he, on more than one occasion, acting in an unofficial capacity, had arranged important treaties between Great Britain and a foreign Power, leaving to ambassadors the arrangements of detail and the final ratification. There were whispers abroad that he was a trusted and tried agent of the British Government, but in exactly what capacity was unknown. His name frequently appeared among the invited guests of Cabinet Ministers, and he received cards for many official functions, but the actual manner in which he rendered assistance to the Government was always kept a most profound secret.

More than once Sir Hugh had mentioned the matter over the dining-table, expressing wonder as to Fetherston's real position.

"You know him well, Enid," he had exclaimed once, laughing over to her. "What is your opinion?"

"I really haven't any," she declared. "His movements are certainly rapid, and often most mysterious."

"He's a most excellent fellow," declared the old general. "Cartwright told me so the other day in the club. Cartwright was ambassador in Petrograd before the war."

Enid remembered this as she stood there, her hands behind her back.

"Before I left I heard that Paul had been called unexpectedly to Paris," he said a few moments later. "Has he returned?"

"Not yet, I believe. I had a letter from Blanche this morning. When it was written, two days ago, he was still absent." Then she added: "There is some mystery regarding his visit to the capital. Blanche left for Paris yesterday, I believe, for she had telegraphed to him, but received no reply."

"She has gone to Paris!" he echoed. "Why did she go? It was silly!"

"Well – because she is puzzled, I think. It was very strange that Paul, even though at the very gate, did not leave those two men and wish her adieu."

"Two men – what two men?" he asked in affected ignorance.

"The two men who stopped the car and demanded to speak with him," she said; and, continuing, described to him that remarkable midnight incident close to the château.

"No doubt he went to Paris upon some important business," Fetherston said, reassuring her. "It was, I think, foolish of his wife to follow. At least, that's my opinion."

He knew that when madame arrived in Paris the ghastly truth must, sooner or later, be revealed.

CHAPTER XX

IN WHICH A TRUTH IS TOLD

As Fetherston sat there, still chatting with his well-beloved, he felt a hatred of himself for being thus compelled to deceive her - to withhold from her the hideous truth of Paul's arrest.

After all, silence was best. If Walter spoke to the girl before him, then he must of necessity reveal his own connection with the affair. He knew she had been puzzled by his presence in France, but his explanation, he hoped, had been sufficient. He had assured her that the only motive of his journey had been to be near her, which was, indeed, no untruth.

He saw that Enid was not altogether at her ease in his presence. Perhaps it was because of those questions and his plain outspokenness when last they met, on that forest road, where they had discussed the strange death of Harry Bellairs.

On that evening, full of suspicion and apprehension, he had decided to tear himself away from her. But, alas! He had found himself powerless to do so. Pity and sympathy filled his heart; therefore, how could he turn from her and abandon her at this moment of her peril? It was on the next day that he had discerned Weirmarsh's sinister intentions. Therefore, he had risen to watch and to combat them.

Some of his suspicions had been confirmed, nevertheless his chief object had not yet been attained - the elucidation of the mystery surrounding the remarkable death of Bellairs.

He was about to refer again to that tragic incident when Enid said suddenly: "Doctor Weirmarsh called and saw Sir Hugh this morning. You told me to tell you when next he called."

"Weirmarsh!" exclaimed the novelist in surprise. "I was not aware that he was in London!"

"He's been abroad - in Copenhagen, I think. He has a brother living there."

"He had a private talk with your stepfather, of course?"

"Yes, as usual, they were in the study for quite a long time - nearly two hours. And," added the girl, "I believe that at last they quarrelled. If they have, I'm awfully glad, for I hate that man!"

"Did you overhear them?" asked Fetherston anxiously, apprehensive lest an open quarrel had actually taken place. He knew well that Josef Blot, alias Weirmarsh, was not a man to be trifled with. If Sir Hugh had served his purpose, as he no doubt had, then he would be betrayed to the police without compunction, just as others had been.

Walter Fetherston grew much perturbed at the knowledge of this quarrel between the pair. His sole aim was to protect Sir Hugh, yet how to act he knew not.

"You did not actually hear any of the words spoken, I suppose?" he inquired of Enid.

"Not exactly, except that I heard my stepfather denounce the doctor as an infernal cur and blackguard."

"Well, and what did Weirmarsh reply?"

"He threatened Sir Hugh, saying, 'You shall suffer for those words - you, who owe everything to me!' I wonder," added the girl, "what he meant by that?"

"Who knows!" exclaimed Walter. "Some secret exists between them. You told me that you suspected it long ago."

"And I do," she said, lowering her voice. "That man holds Sir Hugh in the hollow of his hand - of that I'm sure. I have noticed after each of

135

the doctor's visits how pale and thoughtful he always is."

"Have you tried to learn the reason of it all?" inquired the novelist quietly, his gaze fixed upon her.

"I have," she replied, with slight hesitation.

Walter Fetherston contemplated in silence the fine cat's-eye and diamond ring upon his finger – a ring sent him long ago by an anonymous admirer of his books, which he had ever since worn as a mascot.

At one moment he held this girl in distinct suspicion; at the next, however, he realised her peril, and resolved to stand by her as her champion.

Did he really and honestly love her? He put that question to himself a thousand times. And for the thousandth time was he compelled to answer in the affirmative.

"By which route do you intend travelling to Italy tomorrow?" he asked.

"By Paris and Modane. We go first for a week to Nervi, on the coast beyond Genoa," was her reply.

Fetherston paused. If she put foot in France she would, he knew, be at once placed under arrest as an accomplice of Paul Le Pontois. When Weirmarsh took revenge he always did his work well. No doubt the French police were already at Calais awaiting her arrival.

"I would change the route," he suggested. "Go by Ostend, Strasburg and Milan."

"Mrs. Caldwell has already taken our tickets," she said. "Besides, it is a terribly long way round by that route."

"I know," he murmured. "But it will be best. I have a reason – a strong reason, Enid, for urging you to go by Ostend."

"It is not in my power to do so. Jane always makes our travelling arrangements. Besides, we have sleeping berths secured on the night *rapide* from the Gare de Lyon to Turin."

"I will see Mrs. Caldwell, and get her tickets changed," he said. "Do you understand, Enid? There are reasons - very strong reasons - why you should not travel across France!"

"No, I don't," declared the girl. "You are mysterious again. Why don't you be open with me and give me your reasons for this suggestion?"

"I would most willingly - if I could," he answered. "Unfortunately, I cannot."

"I don't think Mrs. Caldwell will travel by the roundabout route which you suggest merely because you have a whim that we should not cross France," she remarked, looking straight at him.

"If you enter France a disaster will happen - depend upon it," he said, speaking very slowly, his eyes fixed upon her.

"Are you a prophet?" the girl asked. "Can you prophesy dreadful things to happen to us?"

"I do in this case," he said firmly. "Therefore, take my advice and do not court disaster."

"Can't you be more explicit?" she asked, much puzzled by his strange words.

"No," he answered, shaking his head, "I cannot. I only forewarn you of what must happen. Therefore, I beg of you to take my advice and travel by the alternative route - if you really must go to Italy."

She turned towards the fire and, fixing her gaze upon the flames, remained for a few moments in thought, one neat foot upon the marble kerb.

"You really alarm me with all these serious utterances," she said at last, with a faint, nervous laugh.

He rose and stood by her side.

"Look here, Enid," he said, "can't you see that I am in dead earnest?

Have I not already declared that I am your friend, to assist you against that man Weirmarsh?"

"Yes," she replied, "you have."

"Then will you not heed my warning? There is distinct danger in your visit to France – a danger of which you have no suspicion, but real and serious nevertheless. Don't think about spying; it is not that, I assure you."

"How can I avoid it?"

"By pretending to be unwell," he suggested quickly. "You cannot leave with Mrs. Caldwell. Let her go, and you can join her a few days later, travelling by Ostend. The thing is quite simple."

"But –"

"No, you must not hesitate," he declared. "There are no buts. It is the only way."

"Yes; but tell me what terrible thing is to happen to me if I enter France?" she asked, with an uneasy laugh.

The man hesitated. To speak the truth would be to explain all. Therefore he only shook his head and said, "Please do not ask me to explain a matter of which I am not permitted to speak. If you believe me, Enid," he said in a low, pleading voice, "do heed my warning, I beg of you!"

As he uttered these words the handle of the door turned, and Lady Elcombe, warmly clad in furs, came forward to greet the novelist.

"I'm so glad that I returned before you left, Mr. Fetherston," she exclaimed. "We've been to a most dreary play; and I'm simply dying for some tea. Enid, ring the bell, dear, will you?" Then continuing, she added in warm enthusiasm: "Really, Mr. Fetherston, you are quite a stranger! We hoped to see more of you, but my husband and daughter have been away in France – as perhaps you know."

"So Enid has been telling me," replied Walter. "They've been in a most interesting district."

"Enid is leaving us again tomorrow morning," remarked her mother. "They are going to Nervi. You know it, of course, for I've heard you called the living Baedeker, Mr. Fetherston," she laughed.

"Yes," he replied, "I know it - a rather dull little place, with one or two villas. I prefer Santa Margherita, a little farther along the coast - or Rapallo. But," he added, "your daughter tells me she's not well. I hope she will not be compelled to postpone her departure."

"Of course not," said Lady Elcombe decisively. "She must go tomorrow if she goes at all. I will not allow her to travel by herself."

The girl and the man exchanged meaningful glances, and just then Sir Hugh himself entered, greeting his visitor cheerily.

The butler brought in the tea-tray, and as they sat together the two men chatted.

In pretence that he had not been abroad, Walter was making inquiries regarding the district around Haudiomont, which he declared must be full of interest, and asking the general's opinion of the French new fortresses in anticipation of the new war against Germany.

"Since I have been away," said the general, "I have been forced to arrive at the conclusion that another danger may arrive in the very near future. Germany will try and attack France again - without a doubt. The French are labouring under a dangerous delusion if they suppose that Germany would be satisfied with her obscurity."

"Is that really your opinion, Sir Hugh?" asked Fetherston, somewhat surprised.

"Certainly," was the general's reply. "There will be another war in the near future. My opinions have changed of late, my dear Fetherston," Sir Hugh assured him, as he sipped his tea, "and more especially since I went to visit my daughter. I have recently had opportunities of seeing and learning a good deal."

Fetherston reflected. Those words, coming from Sir Hugh, were certainly strange ones.

Walter was handing Enid the cake when the butler entered, bearing a telegram upon a silver salver, which he handed to Sir Hugh.

Tearing it open, he glanced at the message eagerly, and a second later, with blanched face, stood rigid, statuesque, as though turned into stone.

"Why, what's the matter?" asked his wife. "Whom is it from?"

"Only from Blanche," he answered in a low, strained voice. "She is in Paris - and is leaving tonight for London."

"Is Paul coming?" inquired Enid eagerly.

"No," he answered, with a strenuous effort to remain calm. "He - he cannot leave Paris."

The butler, being told there was no answer, bowed and withdrew, but a few seconds later the door reopened, and he announced:

"Dr. Weirmarsh, Sir Hugh!"

CHAPTER XXI

THE WIDENED BREACH

When Sir Hugh entered his cosy study he found the doctor seated at his ease in the big chair by the fire.

"I thought that, being in the vicinity, I would call and see if you've recovered from your - well, your silly fit of irritability," he said, with a grim smile on his grey face as he looked towards the general.

"I have just received bad news - news which I have all along dreaded," replied the unhappy man, the telegram still in his hand. "Paul Le Pontois has been arrested on some mysterious charge - false, without a doubt!"

"Yes," replied Weirmarsh; "it is most unfortunate. I heard it an hour ago, and the real reason of my visit was to tell you of the *contretemps*."

"Someone must have made a false charge against him," cried the general excitedly. "The poor fellow is innocent - entirely innocent! I only have a brief telegram from his wife. She is in despair, and leaves for London tonight."

"My dear Sir Hugh, France is in a very hysterical mood just now. Of course, there must be some mistake. Some private enemy of his has made the charge without a doubt - someone jealous of his position, perhaps. Allegations are easily made, though not so easily substantiated."

"Except by manufactured evidence and forged documents," snapped Sir Hugh. "If Paul is the victim of some political party and is to be made a scapegoat, then Heaven help him, poor fellow. They will never

141

allow him to prove his innocence, unless —"

"Unless what?"

"Unless I come forward," he said very slowly, staring straight before him. "Unless I come forward and tell the truth of my dealings with you. The charges against Paul are false. I know it now. What have you to say?" he added in a low, hard voice.

"A great deal of good that would do!" laughed Weirmarsh, selecting a cigarette from his gold case and lighting it, regarding his host with those narrow-set, sinister eyes of his. "It would only implicate Le Pontois further. They would say, and with truth, that you knew of the whole conspiracy and had profited by it."

"I should tell them what I know concerning you. Indeed, I wrote out a full statement while I was staying with Paul. And I have it ready to hand for the authorities."

"You can do so, of course, if you choose," was the careless reply. "It really doesn't matter to me what statement you make. You have always preserved silence up to the present, therefore I should believe that in this case silence was still golden."

"And you suggest that I stand calmly by and see Le Pontois sentenced to a long term of imprisonment for a crime which he has not committed, eh?"

"I don't suggest anything, my dear Sir Hugh," was the man's reply; "I leave it all to your good judgment."

Since they had met in secret Weirmarsh had made a flying visit to Brussels, where he had conferred with two friends of his. Upon their suggestion he was now acting.

If Paul Le Pontois were secretly denounced and afterwards found innocent, then it would only mystify the French police; the policy pursued towards the Sûreté, as well as towards Sir Hugh, was a clever move on Weirmarsh's part.

"What am I to say to my poor girl when she arrives here in tears tomorrow?" demanded the fine old British officer hoarsely.

"You know that best yourself," was Weirmarsh's brusque reply.

"To you I owe all my recent troubles," the elder man declared. "Because - because," he added bitterly, "you bought me up body and soul."

"A mere business arrangement, wasn't it, Sir Hugh?" remarked his visitor. "Of course, I'm very sorry if any great trouble has fallen upon you on my account. I hope, for instance, you do not suspect me of conspiring to denounce your son-in-law," he added.

"Well, I don't know," was the other's reply; "yet I feel that, in view of this *contretemps*, I must in future break off all connection with you."

"And lose the annual grant which you find so extremely useful?"

"I shall be compelled to do without it. And, at least, I shall have peace of mind."

"Perhaps," remarked the other meaningly.

Sir Hugh realised that this man intended still to hold him in the hollow of his hand. From that one false step he had taken years ago he had never been able to draw back.

Hour by hour, and day by day, had his conscience pricked him. Those chats with the doctor in that grimy little consulting-room in Pimlico remained ever in his memory.

The doctor was the representative of those who held him in their power - persons who were being continually hunted by the police, yet who always evaded them - criminals all! To insult him would be to insult those who had paid him so well for his confidential services.

Yet, filled with contempt for himself, he asked whether he did not deserve to be degraded publicly, and drummed out of the army.

Were it not for Lady Elcombe and Enid he would long ago have gone to East Africa and effaced himself. But he could not bring himself to desert them.

He had satisfied himself that not a soul in England suspected the truth, for, by the Press, he had long ago been declared to be a patriotic Briton, because in his stirring public speeches, when he had put up for Parliament after the armistice, there was always a genuine "John Bull" ring.

The truth was that he remained unsuspected by all – save by one man who had scented the truth. That man was Walter Fetherston!

Walter alone knew the ghastly circumstances, and it was he who had been working to save the old soldier from himself. He did so for two reasons – first, because he was fond of the bluff, fearless old fellow, and, secondly, because he had been attracted by Enid, and intended to rescue her from the evil thraldom of Weirmarsh.

"Why have you returned here to taunt and irritate me again?" snapped Sir Hugh after a pause.

"I came to tell you news which, apparently, you have already received."

"You could well have kept it. You knew that I should be informed in due course."

"Yes – but I – well, I thought you might grow apprehensive perhaps."

"In what direction?"

"That your connection with the little affair might be discovered by the French police. Bézard, the new chief of the Sûreté, is a pretty shrewd person, remember!"

"But, surely, that is not possible, is it?" gasped the elder man in quick alarm.

"No; you can reassure yourself on that point. Le Pontois knows nothing, therefore he can make no statement – unless, of course, your own actions were suspicious."

"They were not – I am convinced of that."

"Then you have no need to fear. Your son-in-law will certainly not endeavour to implicate you. And if he did, he would not be believed," declared the doctor, although he well knew that Bézard was in possession of full knowledge of the whole truth, and that, only by the timely warning he had so mysteriously received, had this man before him and his stepdaughter escaped arrest.

His dastardly plot to secure their ruin and imprisonment had failed. How the girl had obtained wind of it utterly mystified him. It was really in order to discover the reason of their sudden flight that he had made those two visits.

"Look here, Weirmarsh," exclaimed Sir Hugh with sudden resolution, "I wish you to understand that from today, once and for all, I desire to have no further dealings with you. It was, as you have said, a purely business transaction. Well, I have done the dirty, disgraceful work for which you have paid me, and now my task is at an end."

"I hardly think it is, my dear Sir Hugh," replied the doctor calmly. "As I have said before, I am only the mouthpiece – I am not the employer. But I believe that certain further assistance is required – information which you promised long ago, but failed to procure."

"What was that?"

"You recollect that you promised to obtain something – a little tittle-tattle – concerning a lady."

"Yes," snapped the old officer, "oh, Lady Wansford. Let us talk of something else!"

Weirmarsh, who had been narrowly watching the countenance of his victim, saw that he had mentioned a disagreeable subject. He noted how pale were the general's cheeks, and how his thin hands twitched with suppressed excitement.

"I am quite ready to talk of other matters," he answered, "though I deem it but right to refer to my instructions."

"And what are they?"

"To request you to supply the promised information."

"But I can't - *I really can't!*"

"You made a promise, remember. And upon that promise I made you a loan of five hundred pounds."

"I know!" cried the unhappy man, who had sunk so deeply into the mire that extrication seemed impossible. "I know! But it is a promise that I can't fulfil. I won't be your tool any longer. Gad! I won't. Don't you hear me?"

"You must!" declared Weirmarsh, bending forward and looking straight into his eyes.

"I will not!" shouted Sir Hugh, his eyes flashing with quick anger. "Anything but that."

"Why?"

"My efforts in that direction had tragic results on the last occasion."

"Ah!" laughed Weirmarsh. "I see you are superstitious - or something. I did not expect that of you."

"I am not superstitious, Weirmarsh. I only refuse to do what you want. If I gave it to you, it would mean - no I won't - I tell you I won't!"

"Bah! You are growing sentimental!"

"No - I am growing wise. My eyes are at last opened to the dastardly methods of you and your infernal friends. Hear me, once and for all; I refuse to assist you further; and, moreover, I defy you!"

The doctor was silent for a moment, contemplating the ruby on his finger. Then, rising slowly from his chair, he said: "Ah! You do not fully realise what your refusal may cost you."

"Cost what it may, Weirmarsh, I ask you to leave my house at once," said the general, scarlet with anger and beside himself with remorse. "And I shall give orders that you are not again to be admitted here."

"Very good!" laughed the other, with a sinister grin. "You will very soon be seeking me in my surgery."

"We shall see," replied Sir Hugh, with a shrug of his shoulders, as the other strode out of his room.

CHAPTER XXII

CONCERNING THE BELLAIRS AFFAIR

What Walter Fetherston had feared had happened. The two men had quarrelled! Throughout the whole of that evening he watched the doctor's movements.

In any other country but our dear old hood-winked England, Fetherston, in the ordinary course, would have been the recipient of high honours from the Sovereign. But he was a writer, and not a financier. He could not afford to subscribe to the party funds, a course suggested by the flat-footed old Lady G —, who was the tout of Government Whips.

Walter preferred to preserve his independence. He had seen and known much during the war, and, disgusted, he preferred to adopt the Canadian Government's decree and remain without "honours."

His pet phrase was: "The extent of a Party's dishonours is known by the honours it bestows. Scraps of ribbon, 'X.Y.Z.' or O.B.E. Behind one's name can neither make the gentleman nor create the lady."

His secret connection with Scotland Yard, which was purely patriotic and conducted as a student of underground crime, had taught him many strange things, and he had learnt many remarkable secrets. Some of them were, indeed, his secrets before they became secrets of the Cabinet.

Many of those secrets he kept to himself, one being the remarkable truth that General Sir Hugh Elcombe was implicated in a very strange jumble of affairs – a matter that was indeed incredible.

To the tall, well-groomed, military-looking man with whom he stood at eleven o'clock on the following morning – in a private room at New Scotland Yard – he had never confided that discovery of his. To have done so would have been to betray a man who had a brilliant record as a soldier, and who still held high position at the War Office.

By such denunciation he knew he might earn from "the eyes of the Government" very high commendation, in addition to what he had already earned, yet he had resolved, if possible, to save the old officer, who was really more sinned against than sinning.

"You seem to keep pretty close at the heels of your friend, the doctor of Vauxhall Bridge Road!" laughed Trendall, the director of the department, as they stood together in the big, airy, official-looking room, the two long windows of which looked out over Westminster Bridge.

"You've been in France, Montgomery says. What was your friend doing there?"

"He's been there against his will – very much against his will!"

"And you've found out something – eh?"

"Yes," replied Fetherston. "One or two things."

"Something interesting, of course," remarked the shrewd, active, dark-haired man of fifty, under whose control was one of the most important departments of Scotland Yard. "But tell me, in what direction is this versatile doctor of yours working just at the present?"

"I hardly know," was the novelist's reply, as in a navy serge suit he leaned near the window which overlooked the Thames. "I believe some deep scheme is afoot, but at present I cannot see very far. For that reason I am remaining watchful."

"He does not suspect you, of course? If he does, I'd give you Harris, or Charlesworth, or another of the men – in fact, whoever you like – to assist you."

"Perhaps I may require someone before long. If so, I will write or wire to the usual private box at the General Post Office, and shall then be glad if you will send a man to meet me."

"Certainly. It was you, Fetherston, who first discovered the existence of this interesting doctor, who had already lived in Vauxhall Bridge Road for eighteen months without arousing suspicion. You have, indeed, a fine nose for mysteries."

At that moment the telephone, standing upon the big writing-table, rang loudly, and the man of secrets crossed to it and listened.

"It's Heywood – at Victoria Station. He's asking for you," he exclaimed.

Walter went to the instrument, and through it heard the words: "The boat train has just gone, sir. Mrs. Caldwell waited for the young lady until the train went off, but she did not arrive. She seemed annoyed and disappointed. Dr. Weirmarsh has been on the platform, evidently watching also."

"Thanks, Heywood," replied Fetherston sharply; "that was all I wanted to know. Good day."

He replaced the receiver, and, walking back to his friend against the window, explained: "A simple little inquiry I was making regarding a departure by the boat train for Paris – that was all."

But he reflected that if Weirmarsh had been watching it must have been to warn the French police over at Calais of the coming of Enid. No action was too dastardly for that unscrupulous scoundrel.

Yet, for the present at least, the girl remained safe. The chief peril was that in which Sir Hugh was placed, now that he had openly defied the doctor.

On the previous evening he had been in the drawing-room at Hill Street when Sir Hugh had returned from interviewing the caller. By his countenance and manner he at once realised that the breach had been widened.

The one thought by which he was obsessed was how he should save Sir Hugh from disgrace. His connection with the Criminal Investigation Department placed at his disposal a marvellous network of sources of information, amazing as they were unsuspected. He was secretly glad that at last the old fellow had resolved to face bankruptcy rather than go farther in that strange career of crime, yet, at the same time, there was serious danger – for Weirmarsh was a man so unscrupulous and so vindictive that the penalty of his defiance must assuredly be a severe one.

The very presence of the doctor on the platform of the South Eastern station at Victoria that morning showed that he did not intend to allow the grass to grow beneath his feet.

The novelist was still standing near the long window, looking aimlessly down upon the Embankment, with its hurrying foot-passengers and whirling taxis.

"You seem unusually thoughtful, Fetherston," remarked Trendall with some curiosity, as he seated himself at the table and resumed the opening of his letters which his friend's visit had interrupted. "What's the matter?"

"The fact is, I'm very much puzzled."

"About what? You're generally very successful in obtaining solutions where other men have failed."

"To the problem which is greatly exercising my mind just now I can obtain no solution," he said in a low, intense voice.

"What is it? Can I help you?"

"Well," he exclaimed, with some hesitation, "I am still trying to discover why Harry Bellairs died and who killed him."

"That mystery has long ago been placed by us among those which admit of no solution, my dear fellow," declared his friend. "We did our best to throw some light upon it, but all to no purpose. I set the whole of our machinery at work at the time – days before you suspected anything wrong – but not a trace of the truth could we find."

"But what could have been the motive, do you imagine? From all accounts he was a most popular young officer, without a single enemy in the world."

"Jealousy," was the dark man's slow reply. "My own idea is that a woman killed him."

"Why?" cried Walter quickly. "What causes you to make such a suggestion?"

"Well – listen, and when I've finished you can draw your own conclusions."

CHAPTER XXIII

THE SILENCE OF THE MAN BARKER

"Harry Bellairs was an old friend of mine," Trendall went on, leaning back in his padded writing-chair and turning towards where the novelist was standing. "His curious end was a problem which, of course, attracted you as a writer of fiction. The world believed his death to be due to natural causes, in view of the failure of Professors Dale and Boyd, the Home Office analysts, to find a trace of poison or of foul play."

"You believe, then, that he was poisoned?" asked Fetherston quickly.

The other shrugged his shoulders, saying: "How can that point be cleared up? There was no evidence of it."

"It is curious that, though we are both so intensely interested in the problem, we have never before discussed it," remarked Walter. "I am so anxious to hear your views upon one or two points. What, for instance, do you think of Barker, the dead man's valet?"

Herbert Trendall hesitated, and for a moment twisted his moustache. He was a marvellously alert man, an unusually good linguist, and a cosmopolitan to his finger-tips. He had been a detective-sergeant in the T Division of Metropolitan Police for years before his appointment as director of that section. He knew more of the criminal undercurrents on the Continent than any living Englishman, and it was he who furnished accurate information to the Sûreté in Paris concerning the great Humbert swindle.

"Well," he said, "if I recollect aright, the inquiries regarding him were not altogether satisfactory. Previous to his engagement by Harry he had, it seems, been valet to a man named Mitchell, a horse-trainer of rather shady repute."

"Where is he now?"

"I really don't know, but I can easily find out – I gave orders that he was not to be lost sight of." And, scribbling a hasty memorandum, he pressed the electric button upon the arm of his chair.

His secretary, a tall, thin, deep-eyed man, entered, and to him he gave the note.

"Well, let us proceed while they are looking up the information," the chief went on. "Harry Bellairs, as you know, was on the staff of Sir Hugh Elcombe, that dear, harmless old friend of yours who inspects troops and seems to do odd jobs for Whitehall. I knew Harry before he went to Sandhurst; his people, who lived up near Durham, were very civil to me once or twice and gave me some excellent pheasant-shooting. It seems that on that day in September he came up to town from Salisbury – but you know all the facts, of course?"

"I know all the facts as far as they were related in the papers," Walter said. He did not reveal the results of the close independent inquiries he had already made – results which had utterly astounded, and at the same time mystified, him.

"Well," said Trendall, "what the Press published was mostly fiction. Even the evidence given before the coroner was utterly unreliable. It was mainly given in order to mislead the jury and prevent public suspicion that there had been a sensational tragedy – I arranged it so."

"And there had been a tragedy, no doubt?"

"Of course," declared the other, leaning both elbows upon the table before him and looking straight into the novelist's pale face. "Harry came up from Salisbury, the bearer of some papers from Sir Hugh. He duly arrived at Waterloo, discharged his duty, and went to his rooms in

Half Moon Street. Now, according to Barker's story, his master arrived home early in the afternoon, and sent him out on a message to Richmond. He returned a little after five, when he found his master absent."

"That was the account he gave at the inquest," remarked Fetherston.

"Yes; but it was not the truth. On testing the man's story I discovered that at three-eighteen he was in the Leicester Lounge, in Leicester Square, with an ill-dressed old man, who was described as being short and wearing a rusty, old silk hat. They sat at a table near the window drinking ginger-ale, so that the barmaid could not overhear, and held a long and confidential chat."

"He may afterwards have gone down to Richmond," his friend suggested.

"No; he remained there until past four, and then went round to the Café Royal, where he met another man, a foreigner, of about his own age, believed to have been a Swiss, with whom he took a cup of coffee. The man was a stranger at the café, probably a stranger in London. Barker was in the habit of doing a little betting, and I believe the men he met were some of his betting friends."

"Then you disbelieve the Richmond story?"

"Entirely. What seems more than probable is that Harry gave his man the afternoon off because he wished to entertain somebody clandestinely at his rooms - a woman, perhaps. Yet, as far as I've been able to discover, no one in Half Moon Street saw any stranger of either sex go to his chambers that afternoon."

"You said that you believed the motive of the crime - if crime it really was - was jealousy," remarked Fetherston, thoughtfully rubbing his shaven chin.

"And I certainly do. Harry was essentially a lady's man. He was tall, and an extremely handsome fellow, a thorough-going sportsman, an excellent polo player, a perfect dancer, and a splendid rider to hounds. Little wonder was it that he was about to make a very fine match, for only a month before his death he confided to me in secret the fact – a fact known to me alone – that he was engaged to pretty little Lady Blanche Herbert, eldest daughter of the Earl of Warsborough."

"Engaged to Lady Blanche!" echoed the novelist in surprise, for the girl in question was the prettiest of that year's débutantes as well as a great heiress in her own right.

"Yes. Harry was a lucky dog, poor fellow. The engagement, known only to the Warsboroughs and myself, was to have been kept secret for a year. Now, it is my firm opinion, Fetherston, that some other woman, one of Harry's many female friends, had got wind of it, and very cleverly had her revenge."

"Upon what grounds do you suspect that?" asked the other eagerly – for surely the problem was becoming more inscrutable than any of those in the remarkable romances which he penned.

"Well, my conclusions are drawn from several very startling facts – facts which, of course, have never leaked out to the public. But before I reveal them to you I'd like to hear what opinion you've formed yourself."

"I'm convinced that Harry Bellairs met with foul play, and I'm equally certain that the man Barker lied in his depositions before the coroner. He knows the whole story, and has been paid to keep a still tongue."

"There I entirely agree with you," Trendall declared quickly; while at that moment the secretary returned with a slip of paper attached to the query which his chief had written. "Ah!" he exclaimed, glancing at the paper, "I see that the fellow Barker, who was a chauffeur before he entered Harry's service, has set up a motorcar business in Southampton."

"You believe him to have been an accessory, eh?"

"Yes, a dupe in the hands of a clever woman."

"Of what woman?" asked Walter, holding his breath.

"As you know, Harry was secretary to your friend Elcombe. Well, I happen to know that his pretty stepdaughter, Enid Orlebar, was over head and ears in love with him. My daughter Ethel and she are friends, and she confided this fact to Ethel only a month before the tragedy."

"Then you actually suggest that a - a certain woman murdered him?" gasped Fetherston.

"Well - there is no actual proof - only strong suspicion!"

Walter Fetherston held his breath. Did the suspicions of this man, from whom no secret was safe, run in the same direction as his own?

"There was in the evidence given before the coroner a suggestion that the captain had dined somewhere in secret," he said.

"I know. But we have since cleared up that point. He was not given poison while he sat at dinner, for we know that he dined at the Bachelors' with a man named Friend. They had a hurried meal, because Friend had to catch a train to the west of England."

"And afterwards?"

"He left the club in a taxi at eight. But what his movements exactly were we cannot ascertain. He returned to his chambers at a quarter past nine in order to change his clothes and go back to Salisbury, but he was almost immediately taken ill. Barker declares that his master sent him out on an errand instantly on his return, and that when he came in he found him dying."

"Did he not explain what the errand was?"

"No; he refused to say."

In that refusal Fetherston saw that the valet, whatever might be his fault, was loyal to his dead master and to Enid Orlebar. He had not told how Bellairs had sent to Hill Street that scribbled note, and how the distressed girl had torn along to Half Moon Street to arrive too late to speak for the last time with the man she loved. Was Barker an enemy, or was he a friend?

"That refusal arouses distinct suspicion, eh?"

"Barker has very cleverly concealed some important fact," replied the keen-faced man who controlled that section of Scotland Yard. "Bellairs, feeling deadly ill, and knowing that he had fallen a victim to some enemy, sent Barker out for somebody in whom to confide. The man claimed that the errand that his master sent him upon was one of confidence."

"And to whom do you think he was sent?"

"To a woman," was Trendall's slow and serious reply. "To the woman who murdered him!"

"But if she had poisoned him, surely he would not send for her?" exclaimed Fetherston.

"At the moment he was not aware of the woman's jealousy, or of the subtle means used to cause his untimely end. He was unsuspicious of that cruel, deadly hatred lying so deep in the woman's breast. Lady Blanche, on hearing of the death of her lover, was terribly grieved, and is still abroad. She, of course, made all sorts of wild allegations, but in none of them did we find any basis of fact. Yet, curiously enough, her views were exactly the same as my own - that one of poor Harry's lady friends had been responsible for his fatal seizure."

"Then, after all the inquiries you instituted, you were really unable to point to the actual assassin?" asked Fetherston rather more calmly.

"Not exactly unable - unwilling, rather."

"How do you mean unwilling? You were Bellairs' friend!"

"Yes, I was. He was one of the best and most noble fellows who ever wore the King's uniform, and he died by the treacherous hand of a jealous woman - a clever woman who had paid Barker to maintain silence."

"But, if the dying man wished to make a statement, he surely would not have sent for the very person by whose hand he had fallen," Fetherston protested. "Surely that is not a logical conclusion!"

"Bellairs was not certain that his sudden seizure was not due to something he had eaten at the club - remember he was not certain that her hand had administered the fatal drug," replied Trendall. A hard, serious expression rested upon his face. "He had, no doubt, seen her between the moment when he left the Bachelors' and his arrival, a little over an hour afterwards, at Half Moon Street - where, or how, we know not. Perhaps he drove to her house, and there, at her invitation, drank something. Yet, however it happened, the result was the same; she killed him, even though she was the first friend to whom he sent in his distress - killed him because she had somehow learnt of his secret engagement to Lady Blanche Herbert."

"Yours is certainly a remarkable theory," admitted Walter Fetherston. "May I ask the name of the woman to whom you refer?"

"Yes; she was the woman who loved him so passionately," replied Trendall - "Enid Orlebar."

"Then you really suspect her?" asked Fetherston breathlessly.

"Only as far as certain facts are concerned; and that since Harry's death she has been unceasingly interested in the career of the man Barker."

"Are you quite certain of this?" gasped Fetherston.

"Quite; it is proved beyond the shadow of a doubt."

"Then Enid Orlebar killed him?"

"That if she actually did not kill him with her own hand, she at least knew well who did," was the other's cold, hard reply. "She killed him for two reasons; first, because by poor Harry's death she prevented the exposure of some great secret!"

Walter Fetherston made no reply.

Those inquiries, instituted by Scotland Yard, had resulted in exactly the same theory as his own independent efforts - that Harry Bellairs had been secretly done to death by the woman, who, upon her own admission to him, had been summoned to the young officer's side.

CHAPTER XXIV

WHAT THE DEAD MAN LEFT

It was news to Fetherston that Bellairs had dined at his club on that fateful night.

He had believed that Enid had dined with him. He had proved beyond all doubt that she had been to his rooms that afternoon during Barker's absence. That feather from the boa, and the perfume, were sufficient evidence of her visit.

Yet why had Barker remained in the neighbourhood of Piccadilly Circus if sent by his master with a message to Richmond? He could not doubt a single word that Trendall had told him, for the latter's information was beyond question. Well he knew with what care and cunning such an inquiry would have been made, and how every point would have been proved before being reported to that ever active man who was head of that Department of the Home Office that never sleeps.

"What secret do you suggest might have been divulged?" he asked at last after a long pause.

The big room - the Room of Secrets - was silent, for the double windows prevented the noise of the traffic and the "honk" of the taxi horns from penetrating there. Only the low ticking of the clock broke the quiet.

"I scarcely have any suggestion to offer in that direction," was Trendall's slow reply. "That feature of the affair still remains a mystery."

"But cannot this man Barker be induced to make some statement?"

he queried.

"He will scarcely betray the woman to whom he owes his present prosperity, for he is prosperous and has a snug little balance at his bank. Besides, even though we took the matter in hand, what could we do? There is no evidence against him or against the woman. The farcical proceedings in the coroner's court had tied their hands."

"An open verdict was returned?"

"Yes, at our suggestion. But Professors Dale and Boyd failed to find any traces of poison or of foul play."

"And yet there was foul play – that is absolutely certain!" declared the novelist.

"Unfortunately, yes. Poor Bellairs was a brilliant and promising officer, a man destined to make a distinct mark in the world. It was a pity, perhaps, that he was such a lady-killer."

"A pity that he fell victim to what was evidently a clever plot, and yet – yet – I cannot bring myself to believe that your surmise can be actually correct. He surely would never have sent for the very person who was his enemy and who had plotted to kill him – it doesn't seem feasible, does it?"

"Quite as feasible as any of the strange and crooked circumstances which one finds every day in life's undercurrents," was the quiet rejoinder. "Remember, he was very fond of her – fascinated by her remarkable beauty."

"But he was engaged to Lady Blanche?"

"He intended to marry her, probably for wealth and position. The woman a man of Harry's stamp marries is seldom, if ever, the woman he loves," added the chief with a somewhat cynical smile, for he was essentially a man of the world.

"But what secret could Enid Orlebar desire to hide?" exclaimed Fetherston wonderingly. "If he loved her, he certainly would never have threatened exposure."

"My dear fellow, I've told you briefly my own theory - a theory formed upon all the evidence I could collect," replied the tall, dark-eyed man, as he thrust his hands deeply into his trousers pockets and looked straight into the eyes of his friend.

"If you are so certain that Enid Orlebar is implicated in the affair, if not the actual assassin, why don't you interrogate her?" asked Walter boldly.

"Well - well, to tell the truth, our inquiries are not yet complete. When they are, we may be in a better position - we probably shall be - to put to her certain pointed questions. But," he added quickly, "perhaps I ought not to say this, for I know she is a friend of yours."

"What you tell me is in confidence, as always, Trendall," he replied quickly. "I knew long ago that Enid was deeply attached to Bellairs. But much that you have just told me is entirely fresh to me. I must find Barker and question him."

"I don't think I'd do that. Wait until we have completed our inquiries," urged the other. "If Bellairs was killed in so secret and scientific a manner that no trace was left, he was killed with a cunning and craftiness which betrays a jealous woman rather than a man. Besides, there are other facts we have gathered which go further to prove that Enid Orlebar is the actual culprit."

"What are they? Tell me, Trendall."

"No, my dear chap; you are the lady's friend - it is really unfair to ask me," he protested. "Where the usual mysteries are concerned, I'm always open and above-board with you. But in private investigations like this you must allow me to retain certain knowledge to myself."

"But I beg of you to tell me everything," demanded the other. "I have taken an intense interest in the matter, as you have, even though my motive has been of an entirely different character."

"You have no suspicion that Bellairs was in possession of any great secret – a secret which it was to Miss Orlebar's advantage should be kept?"

"No," was the novelist's prompt response. "But I can't see the drift of your question," he added.

"Well," replied the keen, alert man, who, again seated in his writing-chair, bent slightly towards his visitor, "well, as you've asked me to reveal all I know, Fetherston, I will do so, even though I feel some reluctance, in face of the fact that Miss Orlebar is your friend."

"That makes no difference," declared the other firmly. "I am anxious to clear up the mystery of Bellairs' death."

"Then I think that you need seek no farther for the correct solution," replied Trendall quietly, looking into the other's pale countenance. "Your lady friend killed him – *in order to preserve her own secret.*"

"But what was her secret?"

"We have that yet to establish. It must have been a serious one for her to close his lips in such a manner."

"But they were good friends," declared Fetherston. "He surely had not threatened to expose her?"

"I do not think he had. My own belief is that she became madly jealous of Lady Blanche, and at the same time, fearing the exposure of her secret to the woman to whom her lover had become engaged, she took the subtle means of silencing him. Besides —" And he paused without concluding his sentence.

"Besides what?"

"From the first you suspected Sir Hugh's stepdaughter, eh?"

Fetherston hesitated. Then afterwards he nodded slowly in the affirmative.

"Yes," went on Trendall, "I knew all along that you were suspicious.

You made a certain remarkable discovery, eh, Fetherston?"

The novelist started. At what did his friend hint? Was it possible that the inquiries had led to a suspicion of Sir Hugh's criminal conduct? The very thought appalled him.

"I - well, in the course of the inquiries I made I found that the lady in question was greatly attached to the dead man," replied Fetherston rather lamely.

Trendall smiled. "It was to Enid Orlebar that Harry sent when he felt his fatal seizure. Instead of sending for a doctor, he sent Barker to her, and she at once flew to his side, but, alas, too late to remedy the harm she had already caused. When she arrived he was dead!"

Fetherston was silent. He saw that the inquiries made by the Criminal Investigation Department had led to exactly the same conclusion that he himself had formed.

"This is a most distressing thought - that Enid Orlebar is a murderess!" he declared after a moment's pause.

"It is - I admit. Yet we cannot close our eyes to such outstanding facts, my dear chap. Depend upon it that there is something behind the poor fellow's death of which we have no knowledge. In his death your friend Miss Orlebar sought safety. The letter he wrote to her a week before his assassination is sufficient evidence of that."

"A letter!" gasped Fetherston. "Is there one in existence?"

"Yes; it is in our possession; it reveals the existence of the secret."

"But what was its nature?" cried Fetherston in dismay. "What terrible secret could there possibly be that could only be preserved by Bellairs' silence?"

"That's just the puzzle we have to solve - just the very point which has mystified us all along."

And then he turned to his correspondence again, opening his letters one after the other - letters which, addressed to a box at the General

Post Office in the City, contained secret information from various unsuspected quarters at home and abroad.

Suddenly, in order to change the topic of conversation, which he knew was painful to Walter Fetherston, he mentioned the excellence of the opera at Covent Garden on the previous night. And afterwards he referred to an article in that day's paper which dealt with the idea of obtaining exclusive political intelligence through spirit-bureaux. Then, speaking of the labour unrest, Trendall pronounced his opinion as follows:

"The whole situation would be ludicrous were it not urged so persistently as to be a menace not so much in this country, where we know too well the temperaments of its sponsors, but abroad, where public opinion, imperfectly instructed, may imagine it represents a serious national feeling. The continuance of it is an intolerable negation of civilisation; it is supported by no public men of credit; it has been disproved again and again. Ridicule may be left to give the menace the *coup de grâce!* And this," he laughed, "in face of what you and I know, eh? Ah! How long will the British public be lulled to sleep by anonymous scribblers?"

"One day they'll have a rude awakening," declared Fetherston, still thinking, however, of that letter of the dead man to Enid. "I wonder," he added, "I wonder who inspires these denials? We know, of course, that each time anything against enemy interests appears in a certain section of the Press there arises a ready army of letter-writers who rush into print and append their names to assurances that the enemy is nowadays our best friend. Those 'patriotic Englishmen' are, many of them, in high positions.

"When responsible papers wilfully mislead the public, what can be expected?" Walter went on. "But," he added after a pause, "we did not arrive at any definite conclusion regarding the tragic death of Bellairs.

What about that letter of his?"

Trendall was thoughtful for a few minutes.

"My conclusion – the only one that can be formed," he answered at last, disregarding his friend's question – "is that Enid Orlebar is the guilty person; and before long I hope to be in possession of that secret which she strove by her crime to suppress – a secret which I feel convinced we shall discover to be one of an amazing character."

Walter stood motionless as a statue.

Surely Bellairs had not died by Enid's hand!

CHAPTER XXV

AT THE CAFÉ DE PARIS

It was in the early days of January – damp and foggy in England.

Walter Fetherston sat idling on the terrasse of the Café de Paris in Monte Carlo sipping a "mazagran," basking in the afternoon sunshine, and listening to the music of the Rumanian Orchestra.

Around him everywhere was the gay cosmopolitan world of the tables – that giddy little after-the-war financier and profiteer world which amuses itself on the *Côte d'Azur*, and in which he was such a well-known figure.

So many successive seasons had he passed there before 1914 that across at the rooms the attendants and croupiers knew him as an habitué, and he was always granted the *carte blanche* – the white card of the professional gambler. With nearly half the people he met he had a nodding acquaintance, for friendships are easily formed over the *tapis vert* – and as easily dropped.

Preferring the fresher air of Nice, he made his headquarters at the Hôtel Royal on the world-famed promenade, and came over to "Monte" daily by the *rapide*.

Much had occurred since that autumn morning when he had stood with Herbert Trendall in the big room at New Scotland Yard, much that had puzzled him, much that had held him in fear lest the ghastly truth concerning Sir Hugh should be revealed.

His own activity had been, perhaps, unparalleled. The strain of such constant travel and continual excitement would have broken most men; but he possessed an iron constitution, and though he spent weeks on end in trains and steamboats, it never affected him in the least. He could snatch sleep at any time, and he could write anywhere.

Whether or not Enid had guessed the reason of his urgent appeal to her not to pass through France, she had nevertheless managed to excuse herself; but a week after Mrs. Caldwell's departure she had travelled alone by the Harwich-Antwerp route, evidently much to the annoyance of the alert doctor of Pimlico.

Walter had impressed upon her the desirability of not entering France – without, however, giving any plain reason. He left her to guess.

Through secret sources in Paris he had learnt how poor Paul Le Pontois was still awaiting trial. In order not to excite public opinion, the matter was being kept secret by the French authorities, and it had been decided that the inquiry should be held with closed doors.

A week after his arrest the French police received additional evidence against him in the form of a cryptic telegram addressed to the Château, an infamous and easily deciphered message which, no doubt, had been sent with the distinct purpose of strengthening the amazing charge against him. He protested entire ignorance of the sender and of the meaning of the message, but his accusers would not accept any disclaimer. So cleverly, indeed, had the message been worded that at the Sûreté it was believed to refer to the price he had received for certain bundles of spurious notes.

Without a doubt the scandalous telegram had been sent at Weirmarsh's instigation by one of his friends in order to influence the authorities in Paris.

So far as the doctor was concerned he was ever active in receiving reports from his cosmopolitan friends abroad. But since his quarrel with Sir Hugh he had ceased to visit Hill Street, and had, apparently, dropped the old general's acquaintance.

Sir Hugh was congratulating himself at the easy solution of the difficulty, but Walter, seated at that little marble-topped table in the winter sunshine, knowing Weirmarsh's character, remained in daily apprehension.

The exciting life he led in assisting to watch those whom Scotland Yard suspected was as nothing compared with the constant fear of the unmasking of Sir Hugh Elcombe. Doctor Weirmarsh was an enemy, and a formidable one.

The mystery concerning the death of Bellairs had increased rather than diminished. Each step he had taken in the inquiry only plunged him deeper and deeper into an inscrutable problem. He had devoted weeks to endeavouring to solve the mystery, but it remained, alas, inscrutable.

Enid and Mrs. Caldwell had altered their plans, and had gone to Sicily instead of to Egypt, first visiting Palermo and Syracuse, and were at the moment staying at the popular "San Domenico" at Taormina, amid that gem of Mediterranean scenery. Sir Hugh and his wife, much upset by Blanche's sudden arrival in London, had not gone abroad that winter, but had remained at Hill Street to comfort Paul's wife and child.

As for Walter, he had of late been wandering far afield, in Petrograd, Geneva, Rome, Florence, Málaga, and for the past week had been at Monte Carlo. He was not there wholly for pleasure, for, if the truth be told, there were seated at the farther end of the *terrasse* a smartly dressed man and a woman in whom he had for the past month been taking a very keen interest.

This pair, of Swiss nationality, he had watched in half a dozen Continental cities, gradually establishing his suspicions as to their real occupation.

They had come to Monte Carlo for neither health nor pleasure, but in order to meet a grey-haired man in spectacles, whom they received twice in private at the Métropole, where they were staying.

The Englishman had first seen them sitting together one evening at one of the marble-topped tables at the Café Royal in Regent Street, while he had been idly playing a game of dominoes at the next table with an American friend. The face of the man was to him somehow familiar. He felt that he had seen it somewhere, but whether in a photograph in his big album down at Idsworth or in the flesh he could not decide.

Yet from that moment he had hardly lost sight of them. With that astuteness which was Fetherston's chief characteristic, he had watched vigilantly and patiently, establishing the fact that the pair were in England for some sinister purpose. His powers were little short of marvellous. He really seemed, as Trendall once put it, to scent the presence of criminals as pigs scent truffles.

They suddenly left the Midland Hotel at St. Pancras, where they were staying, and crossed the Channel. But the same boat carried Walter Fetherston, who took infinite care not to obtrude himself upon their attention.

Monte Carlo, being in the principality of Monaco, and being peopled by the most cosmopolitan crowd in the whole world, is in winter the recognised meeting-place of chevaliers d'industrie and those who finance and control great crimes.

In the big atrium of those stifling rooms many an assassin has met his hirer, and in many of those fine hotels have bribes been handed over to those who will do "dirty work." It is the European exchange of criminality, for both sexes know it to be a safe place where they may "accidentally" meet the person controlling them.

It is safe to say that in every code used by the criminal plotters of every country in Europe there is a cryptic word which signifies a meeting at Monte Carlo. For that reason was Walter Fetherston much given to idling on the sunny *terrasse* of the café at a point where he could see every person who ascended or descended that flight of red-carpeted stairs which gives entrance to the rooms.

The pair whom he was engaged in watching had been playing at roulette with five-franc pieces, and the woman was now counting her gains and laughing gaily with her husband as she slowly sipped her tea flavoured with orange-flower water. They were in ignorance of the presence of that lynx-eyed man in grey flannels and straw hat who smoked his cigarette leisurely and appeared to be so intensely bored.

No second glance at Fetherston was needed to ascertain that he was a most thorough-going cosmopolitan. He usually wore his pale-grey felt hat at a slight angle, and had the air of the easy-going adventurer, debonair and unscrupulous. But in his case his appearance was not a true index to his character, for in reality he was a steady, hard-headed, intelligent man, the very soul of honour, and, above all, a man of intense patriotism – an Englishman to the backbone. Still, he cultivated his easy-going cosmopolitanism to pose as a careless adventurer.

Presently the pair rose, and, crossing the palm-lined place, entered the casino; while Walter, finishing his "mazagran," lit a fresh cigarette, and took a turn along the front of the casino in order to watch the pigeon-shooting.

The winter sun was sinking into the tideless sea in all its gold-and-orange glory as he stood leaning over the stone balustrade watching the splendid marksmanship of one of the crack shots of Europe. He waited until the contest had ended, then he descended and took the *rapide* back to Nice for dinner.

At nine o'clock he returned to Monte Carlo, and again ascended the station lift, as was his habit, for a stroll through the rooms and a chat and drink with one or other of his many friends. He looked everywhere for the Swiss pair in whom he was so interested, but in vain. Probably they had gone over to Nice to spend the evening, he thought. But as the night wore on and they did not return by the midnight train – the arrival of which he watched – he strolled back to the Métropole and inquired for them at the bureau of the hotel.

"M'sieur and Madame Granier left by the Mediterranean express for Paris at seven-fifteen this evening," replied the clerk, who knew Walter very well.

"What address did they leave?" he inquired, annoyed at the neat manner in which they had escaped his vigilance.

"They left no address, m'sieur. They received a telegram just after six o'clock recalling them to Paris immediately. Fortunately, there was one two-berth compartment vacant on the train."

Walter turned away full of chagrin. He had been foolish to lose sight of them. His only course was to return to Nice, pack his traps, and follow to Paris in the ordinary *rapide* at eight o'clock next morning. And this was the course he pursued.

But Paris is a big place, and though he searched for two whole weeks, going hither and thither to all places where the foreign visitors mostly congregate, he saw nothing of the interesting pair. Therefore, full of disappointment, he crossed one afternoon to Folkestone, and that night again found himself in his dingy chambers in Holles Street.

Next day he called upon Sir Hugh, and found him in much better spirits. Lady Elcombe told him that Enid had written expressing herself delighted with her season in Sicily, and saying that both she and Mrs. Caldwell were very pleased that they had adopted his suggestion of going there instead of to overcrowded Cairo.

As he sat with Sir Hugh and his wife in that pretty drawing-room he knew so well the old general suddenly said: "I suppose, Fetherston, you are still taking as keen an interest in the latest mysteries of crime – eh?"

"Yes, Sir Hugh. As you know, I've written a good deal upon the subject."

"I've read a good many of your books and articles, of course," exclaimed the old officer. "Upon many points I entirely agree with you," he said. "There is a curious case in the papers today. Have you seen it? A young girl found mysteriously shot dead near Hitchin."

"No, I haven't," was Walter's reply. He was not at all interested. He was thinking of something of far greater interest.

CHAPTER XXVI

WHICH IS "PRIVATE AND CONFIDENTIAL"

At eleven o'clock next morning Fetherston stood in Trendall's room at Scotland Yard reporting to him the suspicious movements of Monsieur and Madame Granier.

His friend leaned back in his padded chair listening while the keen-faced man in pince-nez related all the facts, and in doing so showed how shrewd and astute he had been.

"Then they are just what we thought," remarked the chief.

"Without a doubt. In Monte Carlo they received further instructions from somebody. They went to Paris, and there I lost them."

Trendall smiled, for he saw how annoyed his friend was at their escape.

"Well, you certainly clung on to them," he said. "When you first told me your suspicions I confess I was inclined to disagree with you. You merely met them casually in Regent Street. What made you suspicious?"

"One very important incident – Weirmarsh came in with another man, and, in passing, nodded to Granier. That set me thinking."

"But you do not know of any actual dealings with the doctor?"

"I know of none," replied Walter. "Still, I'm very sick that, after all my pains, they should have escaped to Paris so suddenly."

"Never mind," said Trendall. "If they are what we suspect we shall pick them up again before long, no doubt. Now look here," he added. "Read that! It's just come in. As you know, any foreigner who takes a house in certain districts nowadays is reported to us by the local police."

Fetherston took the big sheet of blue official paper which the police official handed to him, and found that it was the copy of a confidential report made by the Superintendent of Police at Maldon, in Essex, and read as follows:

"I, William Warden, Superintendent of Police for the Borough of Maldon, desire to report to the Commissioner of Metropolitan Police the following statement from Sergeant S. Deacon, Essex Constabulary, stationed at Southminster, which is as below:

"'On Friday, the thirteenth of September last, a gentleman, evidently a foreigner, was sent by Messrs. Hare and James, estate agents, of Malden, to view the house known as The Yews, at Asheldham, in the vicinity of Southminster, and agreed to take it for three years in order to start a poultry farm. The tenant entered into possession a week later, when one vanload of furniture arrived from London. Two days later three other vanloads arrived late in the evening, and were unpacked in the stable-yard at dawn. The tenant, whose name is Bailey – but whose letters come addressed "Baily," and are mostly from Belgium – lived there alone for a fortnight, and was afterwards joined by a foreign manservant named Pietro, who is believed to be an Italian. Though more than three months have elapsed, and I have kept observation upon the house – a large one, standing in its own grounds – I have seen no sign of poultry farming, and therefore deem it a matter for a report. – Samuel Deacon, Sergeant, Essex Constabulary.'"

"Curious!" remarked Walter, when he had finished reading it.

"Yes," said Trendall. "There may be nothing in it."

"It should be inquired into!" declared Walter. "I'll take Summers and go down there to have a look round, if you like."

"I wish you would," said the chief. "I'll 'phone Summers to meet you at Liverpool Street Station," he added, turning to the railway guide. "There's a train at one forty-five. Will that suit you?"

"Yes. Tell him to meet me at Liverpool Street – and we'll see who this 'Mr. Baily' really is."

When, shortly after half-past one, the novelist walked on to the platform at Liverpool Street he was approached by a narrow-faced, middle-aged man in a blue serge suit who presented the appearance of a ship's engineer on leave.

As they sat together in a first-class compartment Fetherston explained to his friend the report made by the police officer at Southminster – the next station to Burnham-on-Crouch – whereupon Summers remarked: "The doctor has been down this way once or twice of late. I wonder if he goes to pay this Mr. Baily, or Bailey, a visit?"

"Perhaps," laughed Walter. "We shall see."

The railway ended at Southminster, but on alighting they had little difficulty in finding the small police station, where the local sergeant of police awaited them, having been warned by telephone.

"Well, gentlemen," said the red-faced man, spreading his big hands on his knees as they sat together in a back room, "Mr. Bailey ain't at home just now. He's away a lot. The house is a big one – not too big for the four van-loads of furniture wot came down from London."

"Has he made any friends in the district, do you know?"

"No, not exactly. 'E often goes and 'as a drink at the Bridgewick Arms at Burnham, close by the coastguard station."

Walter exchanged a meaning glance with his assistant.

"Does he receive any visitors?"

"Very few – he's away such a lot. A woman comes down to see him sometimes – his sister, they say she is."

"What kind of a woman?"

"Oh, she's a lady about thirty-five – beautifully dressed always. She generally comes in a dark-green motor-car, which she drives herself. She was a lady driver during the war."

"Do you know her name?"

"Miss Bailey. She's a foreigner, of course."

"Any other visitors?" asked Fetherston, in his quick, impetuous way, as he polished his pince-nez.

"One day, very soon after Mr. Bailey took the house, I was on duty at Southminster Station in the forenoon, and a gentleman and lady arrived and asked how far it was to The Yews, at Asheldham. I directed them the way to walk over by Newmoor and across the brook. Then I slipped 'ome, got into plain clothes, and went along after them by the footpath."

"Why did you do that?" asked Summers.

"Because I wanted to find out something about this foreigner's visitors. I read at headquarters at Maldon the new instructions about reporting all foreigners who took houses, and I wanted to —"

"To show that you were on the alert, eh, Deacon?" laughed the novelist good-humouredly, and he lit a cigarette.

"That's so, sir," replied the big, red-faced man. "Well, I took a short cut over to The Yews, and got there ten minutes before they did. I hid in the hedge on the north side of the house, and saw that as soon as they walked up the drive Mr. Bailey rushed out to welcome them. The lady seemed very nervous, I thought. I know she was an English lady, because she spoke to me at the station."

"What were they like?" inquired Summers. "Describe both of them."

"Well, the man, as far as I can recollect, was about fifty or so, grey-faced, dark-eyed, wearin' a heavy overcoat with astrachan collar and cuffs. He had light grey suède gloves, and carried a gold-mounted malacca cane with a curved handle. The woman was quite young – not more'n twenty, I should think – and very good-lookin'. She wore a neat tailor-made dress of brown cloth, and a small black velvet hat with a big gold buckle. She had a greyish fur around her neck, with a muff to match, and carried a small, dark green leather bag."

Walter stood staring at the speaker. The description was exactly that of Weirmarsh and Enid Orlebar. The doctor often wore an astrachan-trimmed overcoat, while both dress and hat were the same which Enid had worn three months ago!

He made a few quick inquiries of the red-faced sergeant, but the man's replies only served to convince him that Enid had actually been a visitor at the mysterious house.

"You did not discover their names?"

"The young lady addressed her companion as 'Doctor.' That's all I know," was the officer's reply. "For that reason I was rather inclined to think that I was on the wrong scent. The man was perhaps, after all, only a doctor who had come down to see his patient."

"Perhaps so," remarked Walter mechanically. "You say Mr. Bailey is not at home today, so we'll just run over and have a look round. You'd better come with us, sergeant."

"Very well, sir. But I 'ear as how Mr. Bailey is comin' home this evenin'. I met Pietro in the Railway Inn at Southminster the night before last, and casually asked when his master was comin' home, as I wanted to see 'im for a subscription for our police concert, and 'e told me that the signore – that's what 'e called him – was comin' home tonight."

"Good! Then, after a look round the place, we hope to have the pleasure of seeing this mysterious foreigner who comes here to the Dengie Marshes to make a living out of fowl-keeping." And Walter smiled meaningly at his companion.

Ten minutes later, after the sergeant had changed into plain clothes, the trio set out along the flat, muddy road for Asheldham.

But as they were walking together, after passing Northend, a curious thing happened.

Summers started back suddenly and nudged the novelist's arm without a word.

Fetherston, looking in the direction indicated, halted, utterly staggered by what met his gaze.

It was inexplicable - incredible! He looked again, scarcely believing his own eyes, for what he saw made plain a ghastly truth.

He stood rigid, staring straight before him.

Was it possible that at last he was actually within measurable distance of the solution of the mystery?

CHAPTER XXVII

THE RESULT OF INVESTIGATION

As the expectant trio had come round the bend in the road they saw in front of them, walking alone, a young lady in a short tweed suit with hat to match.

The gown was of a peculiar shade of grey, and by her easy, swinging gait and the graceful carriage of her head Walter Fetherston instantly recognised that there before him, all unconscious of his presence, was the girl he believed to be still in Sicily – Enid Orlebar!

He looked again, to satisfy himself that he was not mistaken. Then, drawing back, lest her attention should be attracted by their footsteps, he motioned to his companions to retreat around the bend and thus out of her sight.

"Now," he said, addressing them, "there is some deep mystery here. That lady must not know we are here."

"You've recognised her, sir?" asked Summers, who had on several previous occasions assisted him.

"Yes," was the novelist's hard reply. "She is here with some mysterious object. You mustn't approach The Yews till dark."

"Mr. Bailey will then be at home, sir," remarked the sergeant. "I thought you wished to explore the place before he arrived?"

Walter paused. He saw that Enid could not be on her way to visit Bailey, if he were not at home. So he suggested that Summers, whom she did not know, should go forward and watch her movements, while he and the sergeant should proceed to the house of suspicion.

Arranging to meet later, the officer from Scotland Yard lit his pipe and strolled quickly forward around the bend to follow the girl in grey, while the other two halted to allow them to get on ahead.

"Have you ever seen that lady down here before, sergeant?" asked Walter presently.

"Yes, sir. If I don't make a mistake, it is the same lady who asked me the way to The Yews soon after Mr. Bailey took the house – the lady who came with the man whom she addressed as 'Doctor'!"

"Are you quite certain of this?"

"Not quite certain. She was dressed differently, in brown – with a different hat and a veil."

"They came only on that one occasion, eh?"

"Only that once, sir."

"But why, I wonder, is she going to The Yews? Pietro, you say, went up to London this morning?"

"Yes, sir, by the nine-five. And the house is locked up – she's evidently unaware of that."

"No doubt. She'll go there, and, finding nobody at home, turn away disappointed. She must not see us."

"We'll take good care of that, sir," laughed the local sergeant breezily, as he left his companion's side and crossed the road so that he could see the bend. "Why!" he exclaimed, "she ain't goin' to Asheldham after all! She's taken the footpath to the left that leads into Steeple! Evidently she knows the road!"

"Then we are free to go straight along to The Yews, eh? She's making a call in the vicinity. I wonder where she's going?"

"Your friend will ascertain that," said the sergeant. "Let's get along to The Yews and 'ave a peep round."

Therefore the pair, now that Enid was sufficiently far ahead along a footpath which led under a high, bare hedge, went forth again down the high road until, after crossing the brook, they turned to the right into Asheldham village, where, half-way between that place and New Hall, they turned up a short by-road, a cul-de-sac, at the end of which a big, old-fashioned, red-brick house of the days of Queen Anne, half hidden by a belt of high Scotch firs, came into view.

Shut off from the by-road by a high, time-mellowed brick wall, it stood back lonely and secluded in about a couple of acres of well wooded ground. From a big, rusty iron gate the ill-kept, gravelled drive took a broad sweep up to the front of the house, a large, roomy one with square, inartistic windows and plain front, the ugliness of which the ivy strove to hide.

In the grey light of that wintry afternoon the place looked inexpressibly dismal and neglected. Years ago it had, no doubt, been the residence of some well-to-do county family; but in these twentieth-century post-war days, having been empty for nearly ten years, it had gone sadly to rack and ruin.

The lawns had become weedy, the carriage-drive was, in places, green with moss, like the sills of the windows and the high-pitched, tiled roof itself. In the centre of the lawn, before the house, stood four great ancient yews, while all round were high box hedges, now, alas, neglected; untrimmed and full of holes.

The curtains were of the commonest kind, while the very steps leading to the front door were grey with lichen and strewn with wisps of straw. The whole aspect was one of neglect, of decay, of mystery.

The two men, opening the creaking iron gate, advanced boldly to the door, an excuse ready in case Pietro opened it.

They knocked loudly, but there was no response. Their summons echoed through the big hall, causing Walter to remark:

"There can't be much furniture inside, judging from the sound."

"Four motor vanloads came here," responded the sergeant. "The first was in a plain van."

"You did not discover whence it came?"

"I asked the driver down at the inn at Southminster, and he told me that they came from the Trinity Furnishing Company, Peckham. But, on making inquiries, I found that he lied; there is no such company in Peckham."

"You saw the furniture unloaded?"

"I was about here when the first lot came. When the other three vans arrived I was away on my annual leave," was the sergeant's reply.

Again they knocked, but no one came to the door. A terrier approached, but he proved friendly, therefore they proceeded to make an inspection of the empty stabling and disused outbuildings.

Three old hen-coops were the only signs of poultry-farming they could discover, and these, placed in a conspicuous position in the big, paved yard, were without feathered occupants.

There were three doors by which the house could be entered, and all of them Walter tried and found locked. Therefore, noticing in the rubbish-heap some stray pieces of paper, he at once turned his attention to what he discovered were fragments of a torn letter. It was written in French, and, apparently, had reference to certain securities held by the tenant of The Yews.

But as only a small portion of the destroyed communication could be found, its purport was not very clear, and the name and address of the writer could not be ascertained.

Yet it had already been proved without doubt that the mysterious tenant of the dismal old place – the man who posed as a poultry-farmer – had had as visitors Dr. Weirmarsh and Enid Orlebar!

For a full half-hour, while the red-faced sergeant kept watch at the gate, Walter Fetherston continued to investigate that rubbish-heap, which showed signs of having been burning quite recently, for most of the scraps of paper were charred at their edges.

The sodden remains of many letters he withdrew and tried to read, but the scraps gave no tangible result, and he was just about to relinquish his search when his eye caught a scrap of bright blue notepaper of a familiar hue. It was half burned, and blurred by the rain, but at the corner he recognised some embossing in dark blue – familiar embossing it was – of part of the address in Hill Street!

The paper was that used habitually by Enid Orlebar, and upon it was a date, two months before, and the single word "over" in her familiar handwriting.

He took his stout walking-stick, in reality a sword-case, and frantically searched for other scraps, but could find none. One tiny portion only had been preserved from the flames – paraffin having been poured over the heap to render it the more inflammable. But that scrap in itself was sufficient proof that Enid had written to the mysterious tenant of The Yews.

"Well," he said at last, approaching the sergeant, "do you think the coast is clear enough?"

"For what?"

"To get a glimpse inside. There's a good deal more mystery here than we imagine, depend upon it!" Walter exclaimed.

"Master and man will return by the same train, I expect, unless they come back in a motor-car. If they come by train they won't be here till well past eight, so we'll have at least three hours by ourselves."

Walter Fetherston glanced around. Twilight was fast falling.

"It'll be dark inside, but I've brought my electric torch," he said. "There's a kitchen window with an ordinary latch."

"That's no use. There are iron bars," declared the sergeant. "I examined it the other day. The small staircase window at the side is the best means of entry." And he took the novelist round and showed him a long narrow window about five feet from the ground.

Walter's one thought was of Enid. Why had she written to that mysterious foreigner? Why had she visited there? Why, indeed, was she back in England surreptitiously, and in that neighbourhood?

The short winter's afternoon was nearly at an end as they stood contemplating the window prior to breaking in – for Walter Fetherston felt justified in breaking the law in order to examine the interior of that place.

In the dark branches of the trees the wind whistled mournfully, and the scudding clouds were precursory of rain.

"Great Scott!" exclaimed Walter. "This isn't a particularly cheerful abode, is it, sergeant?"

"No, sir, if I lived 'ere I'd have the blues in a week," laughed the man. "I can't think 'ow Mr. Bailey employs 'is time."

"Poultry-farming," laughed Fetherston, as, standing on tiptoe, he examined the window-latch by flashing on the electric torch.

"No good!" he declared. "There's a shutter covered with new sheet-iron behind."

"It doesn't show through the curtain," exclaimed Deacon.

"But it's there. Our friend is evidently afraid of burglars."

From window to window they passed, but the mystery was considerably increased by the discovery that at each of those on the ground floor were iron-faced shutters, though so placed as not to be noticeable behind the windows, which were entirely covered with cheap curtain muslin.

"That's funny!" exclaimed the sergeant. "I've never examined them with a light before."

"They have all been newly strengthened," declared Fetherston. "On the other side I expect there are strips of steel placed lattice-wise, a favourite device of foreigners. Mr. Bailey," he added, "evidently has no desire that any intruder should gain access to his residence."

"What shall we do?" asked Deacon, for it was now rapidly growing dark.

A thought had suddenly occurred to Walter that perhaps Enid's intention was to make a call there, after all.

"Our only way to obtain entrance is, I think, by one of the upper windows," replied the man whose very life was occupied by the investigation of mysteries. "In the laundry I noticed a ladder. Let us go and get it."

So the ladder, a rather rotten and insecure one, was obtained, and after some difficulty placed against the wall. It would not, however, reach to the windows, as first intended, therefore Walter mounted upon the slippery, moss-grown tiles of a wing of the house, and after a few moments' exploration discovered a skylight which proved to be over the head of the servants' staircase.

This he lifted, and, fixing around a chimney-stack a strong silk rope he had brought in his pocket ready for any emergency, he threw it down the opening, and quickly lowered himself through.

Scarcely had he done so, and was standing on the uncarpeted stairs, when his quick ear caught the sound of Deacon's footsteps receding over the gravel around to the front of the house.

Then, a second later, he heard a loud challenge from the gloom in a man's voice that was unfamiliar:

"Who's there?"

There was no reply. Walter listened with bated breath.

"What are you doing there?" cried the newcomer in a voice in which was a marked foreign accent. "Speak! *Speak!* Or I'll shoot!"

CHAPTER XXVIII

THE SECRET OF THE LONELY HOUSE

Walter did not move. He realised that a *contretemps* had occurred. The ladder still leaning against the wall outside would reveal his intrusion. Yet, at last inside, he intended, at all hazards, to explore the place and learn the reason why the mysterious stranger had started that "poultry farm."

He was practically in the dark, fearing to flash on his torch lest he should be discovered.

Was it possible that Bailey or his Italian manservant had unexpectedly returned!

Those breathless moments seemed hours.

Suddenly he heard a second challenge. The challenger used a fierce Italian oath, and by it he knew that it was Pietro.

In reply, a shot rang out - evidently from the sergeant's pistol, followed by another sharp report, and still another. This action showed the man Deacon to be a shrewd person, for the effect was exactly as he had intended. The Italian servant turned on his heel and flew for his life down the drive, shouting in his native tongue for help and for the police.

"Madonna santa!" he yelled. "Who are you here?" he demanded in Italian. "I'll go to the police!"

And in terror he rushed off down the road.

"All right, sir," cried the sergeant, after the servant had disappeared.

"I've given the fellow a good fright. Be quick and have a look round, sir. You can be out again before he raises the alarm!"

In an instant Walter flashed on his torch and, dashing down the stairs, crossed the kitchen and found himself in the hall. From room to room he rushed, but found only two rooms on the ground floor furnished – a sitting-room, which had been the original dining-room, while in the study was a chair-bed, most probably where Pietro slept.

On the table lay a heavy revolver, fully loaded, and this Fetherston quickly transferred to his jacket pocket.

Next moment he dashed up the old well staircase two steps at a time and entered room after room. Only one was furnished – the tenant's bedroom. In it he found a number of suits of clothes, while on the dressing-table lay a false moustache, evidently for disguise. A small writing-table was set in the window, and upon it was strewn a quantity of papers.

As he flashed his torch round he was amazed to see, arranged upon a neat deal table in a corner, some curious-looking machinery which looked something like printing-presses. But they were a mystery to him.

The discovery was a strange one. What it meant he did not then realise. There seemed to be quite a quantity of apparatus and machinery. It was this which had been conveyed there in those furniture vans of the Trinity Furnishing Company.

He heard Deacon's voice calling again. Therefore, having satisfied himself as to the nature of the contents of that neglected old house, he ascended the stone steps into the passage which led through a faded green-baize door into the main hall.

As he entered he heard voices in loud discussion. Sergeant Deacon and the servant Pietro had met face to face.

The Italian had evidently aroused the villagers in Asheldham, for there were sounds of many voices of men out on the gravelled drive.

"I came up here a quarter of an hour ago," the Italian cried excitedly in his broken English, "and somebody fired at me. They tried to kill me!"

"But who?" asked Deacon in pretended ignorance. He was uncertain what to do, Mr. Fetherston being still within the house and the ladder, his only means of escape, still standing against a side wall.

"Thieves!" cried the man, his foreign accent more pronounced in his excitement. "I challenged them, and they fired at me. I am glad that you, a police sergeant, are here."

"So am I," cried Walter Fetherston, suddenly throwing open the front door and standing before the knot of alarmed villagers, though it was so dark that they could not recognise who he was. "Deacon," he added authoritatively, "arrest that foreigner."

"Diavolo! Who are you?" demanded the Italian angrily.

"You will know in due course," replied Fetherston. Then, turning to the crowd, he added: "Gentlemen, I came here with Sergeant Deacon to search this house. He will tell you whether that statement is true or not."

"Quite," declared the breezy sergeant, who already had the Italian by the collar and coat-sleeve. "It was I who fired – to frighten him off!"

At this the crowd laughed. They had no liking for foreigners of any sort after the war, and were really secretly pleased to see that the sergeant had "taken him up."

But what for? they asked themselves. Why had the police searched The Yews? Mr. Bailey was a quiet, inoffensive man, very free with his money to everybody around.

"Jack Beard," cried Deacon to a man in the crowd, "just go down to Asheldham and telephone Superintendent Warden at Maldon. Ask him to send me over three men at once, will you?"

"All right, Sam," was the prompt reply, and the man went off, while the sergeant took the resentful Italian into the house to await an escort.

Deacon called the assistance of two men and invited them in. Then, while they mounted guard over the prisoner, Fetherston addressed the little knot of amazed men who had been alarmed by the Italian's statement.

"Listen, gentlemen," he said. "We shall in a couple of hours' time expect the return of Mr. Bailey, the tenant of this house. There is a very serious charge against him. I therefore put everyone of you upon your honour to say no word of what has occurred here tonight – not until Mr. Bailey arrives. I should prefer you all to remain here and wait; otherwise, if a word be dropped at Southminster, he may turn back and fly from justice."

"What's the charge, sir?" asked one man, a bearded old labourer.

"A very serious one," was Walter's evasive reply.

Then, after a pause, they all agreed to wait and witness the dramatic arrest of the man who was charged with some mysterious offence. Speculation was rife as to what it would be, and almost every crime in the calendar was cited as likely.

Meanwhile Fetherston, returning to the barely-furnished sitting-room, interrogated Pietro in Italian, but only obtained sullen answers. A loaded revolver had been found upon him by Deacon, and promptly confiscated.

"I have already searched the place," Walter said to the prisoner, "and I know what it contains."

But in response the man who had posed as servant, but who, with his "master," was the custodian of the place, only grinned and gave vent to muttered imprecations in Italian.

Fetherston afterwards left the small assembly and made examination of some bedrooms he had not yet inspected. In three of these, the locks of which he broke open, he discovered quantities of interesting papers, together with another mysterious-looking press.

While trying to decide what it all meant he suddenly heard a great shouting and commotion outside, and ran down to the door to ascertain its cause.

As he opened it he saw that in the darkness the crowd outside had grown excited.

"'Ere you are, sir," cried one man, ascending the steps. "'Ere are two visitors. We found 'em comin' up the road, and, seein' us, they tried to get away!"

Walter held up a hurricane lantern which he had found and lit, when its dim, uncertain light fell upon the two prisoners in the crowd.

Behind stood Summers, while before him, to Fetherston's utter amazement, showed Enid Orlebar, pale and terrified, and the grey, sinister face of Doctor Weirmarsh.

CHAPTER XXIX

CONTAINS SOME STARTLING STATEMENTS

Enid, recognising Walter, shrank back instantly in fear and shame, while Weirmarsh started at that unexpected meeting with the man whom he knew to be his bitterest and most formidable opponent.

The small crowd of excited onlookers, ignorant of the true facts, but their curiosity aroused by the unusual circumstances, had prevented the pair from turning back and making a hurried escape.

"Enid!" exclaimed Fetherston, as the girl reluctantly crossed the threshold with downcast head, "What is the meaning of this? Why are you paying a visit to this house at such an hour?"

"Ah, Walter," she cried, her small, gloved hands clenched with a sudden outburst of emotion, "be patient and hear me! I will tell you everything – *everything!*"

"You won't," growled the doctor sharply. "If you do, by Gad, it will be the worse for you! So you'd best keep a silent tongue – otherwise you know the consequences. I shall now tell the truth – and you won't like that!"

She drew back in terror of the man who held such an extraordinary influence over her. She had grasped Fetherston's hand convulsively, but at Weirmarsh's threat she had released her hold and was standing in the hall, pale, rigid and staring.

"Summers," exclaimed Fetherston, turning to his companion, "you know this person, eh?"

"Yes, sir, I should rather think I do," replied the man, with a grin.

"Well, detain him for the present, and take your instructions from London."

"You have no power or right to detain me," declared the grey-faced doctor in quick defiance. "You are not a police officer!"

"No, but this is a police officer," Fetherston replied, indicating Summers, and adding: "Sergeant, I give that man into custody."

The sergeant advanced and laid his big hand upon the doctor's shoulder, telling him to consider himself under arrest.

"But this is abominable - outrageous!" Weirmarsh cried, shaking him off. "I've committed no offence."

"That is a matter for later consideration," calmly replied the man who had devoted so much of his time and money to the investigation of mysteries of crime.

In one of the bare bedrooms upstairs Fetherston had, in examining one of the well made hand-presses set up there, found beside it a number of one-pound Treasury notes. In curiosity he took one up, and found it to be in an unfinished state. It was printed in green, without the brown colouring. Yet it was perfect as regards the paper and printing - even to its black serial number.

Next second the truth flashed upon him. The whole apparatus, presses and everything, had been set up there to print the war paper currency of Great Britain!

In the room adjoining he had seen bundles of slips of similar paper, all neatly packed in elastic bands, and waiting the final process of colouring and toning. One bundle had only the Houses of Parliament printed; the other side was blank. He saw in a flash that the placing in circulation of such a huge quantity of Treasury notes, amounting to hundreds of thousands of pounds, must seriously damage the credit of the nation.

For a few seconds he held an unfinished note in his hand examining it, and deciding that the imitation was most perfect. It deceived him and would undoubtedly deceive any bank-teller.

In those rooms it was plain that various processes had been conducted, from the manipulation of the watermark, by a remarkably ingenious process, right down to the finished one-pound note, so well done that not even an expert could detect the forgery. There were many French one-hundred-franc notes as well.

The whole situation was truly astounding. Again the thought hammered home: such a quantity of paper in circulation must affect the national finances of Britain. And at the head of the band who were printing and circulating those spurious notes was the mysterious medical man who carried on his practice in Pimlico!

The scene within the sparsely furnished house containing those telltale presses was indeed a weird one.

Somebody had found a cheap paraffin lamp and lit it in the sitting-room, where they were all assembled, the front door having been closed.

It was apparent that Pietro was no stranger to the doctor and his fair companion, but both men were highly resentful that they had been so entrapped.

"Doctor Weirmarsh," exclaimed Fetherston seriously, as he stood before him, "I have just examined this house and have ascertained what it contains."

"You've told him!" cried the man, turning fiercely upon Enid. "You have betrayed me! Ah! It will be the worse for you – and for your family," he added harshly. "You will see! I shall now reveal the truth concerning your stepfather, and you and your family will be held up to opprobrium throughout the whole length and breadth of your land."

Enid did not reply. She was pale as death, her face downcast, her lips white as marble. She knew, alas, that Weirmarsh, now that he was cornered, would not spare her.

There was a pause – a very painful pause.

Everyone next instant listened to a noise which sounded outside. As it grew nearer it grew more distinct – the whir of an approaching motor-car.

It pulled up suddenly before the door, and a moment later the old bell clanged loudly through the half-empty house.

Fetherston left the room, and going to the door, threw it open, when yet another surprise awaited him.

Upon the steps stood four men in thick overcoats, all of whom Walter instantly recognised.

With Trendall stood Sir Hugh Elcombe, while their companions were two detective-inspectors from Scotland Yard.

"Hallo! – Fetherston!" gasped Trendall. "I – I expected to find Weirmarsh here! What has happened?"

"The doctor is already here," was the other's quick reply. "I have found some curious things in this place! Secret printing-presses for forged notes."

"We already know that," he said. "Sir Hugh Elcombe here has, unknown to us, obtained certain knowledge, and today he came to me and gave me a full statement of what has been in progress. What he has told me this afternoon is among the most valuable and reliable information that we ever received."

"I know something of the scoundrels," remarked the old general, "because – well, because, as I have confessed to Mr. Trendall, I yielded to temptation long ago and assisted them."

"Whatever you have done, Sir Hugh, you have at least revealed to us the whole plot. Only by pretending to render assistance to these scoundrels could you have gained the intensely valuable knowledge

196

which you've imparted to me today," replied the keen-faced director from Scotland Yard.

Fetherston realised instantly that the fine old fellow, whom he had always held in such esteem, was making every effort to atone for his conduct in the past; but surely that was not the moment to refer to it – so he ushered the four men into the ill-lit dining-room wherein the others were standing, none knowing how next to act.

When the doctor and Sir Hugh faced each other there was a painful silence for a few seconds.

To Weirmarsh Trendall was known by sight, therefore the criminal saw that the game was up, and that Sir Hugh had risked his own reputation in betraying him.

"You infernal scoundrel!" cried the doctor angrily. "You – to whom I have paid so many thousands of pounds – have given me away! But I'll be even with you!"

"Say what you like," laughed the old general in defiance. "To me it is the same whatever you allege. I have already admitted my slip from the straight path. I do not deny receiving money from your hands, nor do I deny that, in a certain measure, I have committed serious offences – because, having taken one step, you forced me on to others, always holding over me the threat of exposure and ruin. But, fortunately, one day, in desperation, I took Enid yonder into my confidence. It was she who suggested that I might serve the ends of justice, and perhaps atone for what I had already done, by learning your secrets, and, when the time was ripe, revealing all the interesting details to our authorities. Enid became your friend and the friend of your friends. She risked everything – her honour, her happiness, her future – by associating with you for the one and sole purpose of assisting me to learn all the dastardly plot in progress."

"It was you who supplied Paul Le Pontois with the false notes he passed in France!" declared Weirmarsh. "The French police know that; and if ever you or your step-daughter put foot in France you will be arrested."

"Evidently you are unaware, Doctor, that my son-in-law, Paul Le Pontois, was released yesterday," laughed Sir Hugh in triumph. "Your treachery, which is now known by the Sûreté, defeated its own ends."

"Further," remarked Walter Fetherston, turning to Enid, "it was this man here" - and he indicated the grey-faced doctor of Pimlico - "this man who denounced you and Sir Hugh to the French authorities, and had you not heeded my warning you both would then have been arrested. He had evidently suspected the object of your friendliness with me - that you both intended to reveal the truth - and he adopted that course in order to secure your incarceration in a foreign prison, and so close your lips."

"I knew you suspected me all along, Walter," replied the girl, standing a little aside and suddenly clutching his hand. "But you will forgive me now - forgive me, won't you?" she implored, looking up into his dark, determined face.

"Of course," he replied, "I have already forgiven you. I had no idea of the true reason of your association with this man."

And he raised her gloved hand and carried it gallantly to his eager lips.

"Though more than mere suspicion has rested upon you," he went on, "you and your stepfather deserve the heartiest thanks of the nation for risking everything in order to be in a position to reveal this dastardly financial plot. That man there" - and he indicated the doctor - "deserves all he'll get!"

The doctor advanced threateningly, and, drawing a big automatic revolver from his pocket, would have fired at the man who had spoken his mind so freely had not Deacon, quick as lightning, sprung forward and wrenched the weapon so that the bullet went upward.

White with anger and chagrin, the doctor stood roundly abusing the man who had investigated that lonely house.

But Fetherston laughed, which only irritated him the more. He raved like a caged lion, until the veins in his brow stood out in great knots; but, finding all protests and allegations useless, he at last became quiet again, and apparently began to review the situation from a purely philosophical standpoint, until, some ten minutes later, another motor-car dashed up and in it were an inspector and four plain-clothes constables, who had been sent over from Maldon in response to Deacon's message for assistance.

When they entered Pietro became voluble, but the narrow-eyed doctor of Pimlico remained sullen and silent, biting his lips. He saw that he had been entrapped by the very man whom he had believed to be as clay in his hands.

The scene was surely exciting as well as impressive. The half-furnished, ill-lit dining-room was full of excited men, all talking at once.

Unnoticed, Walter drew Enid into the shadow, and in a few brief, passionate words reassured her of his great affection.

"Ah!" she cried, bursting into hot tears, "your words, Walter, have lifted a great load of sorrow and apprehension from my mind, for I feared that when you knew the truth you would never, never forgive."

"But I have forgiven," he whispered, pressing her hand.

"Then wait until we are alone, and I will tell you everything. Ah! You do not know, Walter, what I have suffered – what a terrible strain I have sustained in these days of terror!"

But scarcely had she uttered those words when the door re-opened and a man was ushered in by Deacon, who had gone out in response to the violent ringing of the bell.

"This is Mr. Bailey, tenant of the house, gentlemen," said the sergeant, introducing him with mock politeness.

Fetherston glanced up, and to his surprise saw standing in the doorway a man he had known, and whose movements he had so closely followed – the man who had gone to Monte Carlo for instructions, and perhaps payment – the man who had passed as Monsieur Granier!

CHAPTER XXX

REVEALS A WOMAN'S LOVE

Great was the consternation caused in the neighbourhood of the sleepy old-world village of Asheldham when it became known that the quiet, mild-mannered tenant of The Yews had been arrested by the Maldon police.

Of what transpired within those grim walls only the two men called to his assistance by Sergeant Deacon knew, and to them both the inspector from Maldon, as well as Trendall, expressed a fervent hope that they would regard the matter as strictly confidential.

"You see, gentlemen," added Trendall, "we are not desirous that the public should know of our discovery. We wish to avoid creating undue alarm, and at the same time to conceal the very existence of our system of surveillance upon those suspected. Therefore, I trust that all of you present will assist my department by preserving silence as to what has occurred here this evening."

His hearers agreed willingly, and through the next hour the place was thoroughly searched, the bundles of spurious notes – the finished ones representing nearly one hundred thousand pounds ready to put into circulation – being seized.

One of the machines they found was for printing in the serial numbers in black, a process which, with genuine notes, is done by hand. Truly, the gang had brought the art of forgery to perfection.

"Well," said Trendall when they had finished, "this work of yours, Sir

Hugh, certainly deserves the highest commendation. You have accomplished what we, with all our great organisation, utterly failed to do."

"I have today tried to atone for my past offences," was the stern old man's hoarse reply.

"And you have succeeded, Sir Hugh," declared Trendall. "Indeed you have!"

Shortly afterwards the excitement among the crowd waiting outside in the light of the head-lamps of the motor-cars was increased by the appearance of the doctor, escorted by two Maldon police officers in plain clothes. They mounted a police car, and were driven away down the road, while into a second car the tenant of The Yews and his Italian manservant were placed under escort, and also driven away.

The station-fly, in which Bailey had driven from Southminster, conveyed away Fetherston, Trendall, Sir Hugh, and Enid, while Deacon, with two men, was left in charge of the house of secrets.

It was past one o'clock in the morning when Walter Fetherston stood alone with Enid in the pretty drawing-room in Hill Street.

They stood together upon the vieux rose hearthrug, his hand was upon her shoulder, his deep, earnest gaze fixed upon hers. In her splendid eyes the love light showed. They had both admired each other intensely from their first meeting, and had become very good and staunch friends. Walter Fetherston had only once spoken of the passion that had constantly consumed his heart – when they were by the blue sea at Biarritz. He loved her – loved her with the whole strength of his being – and yet, ah! Try how he would, he could never put aside the dark cloud of suspicion which, as the days went by, became more and more impenetrable.

Sweet-faced, frank, and open, she stood, the ideal of the English outdoor girl, merry, quick-witted, and athletic. And yet, after the stress of war, she had sacrificed all that she held most dear in order to become the friend of Weirmarsh. Why?

"Enid," he said at last, his tender hand still upon her shoulder, "why did you not tell me your true position? You were working in the same direction, with the same strong motive of patriotism, as myself!"

She was silent, very pale, and very serious.

"I feared to tell you, Walter," she faltered. "How could I possibly reveal to you the truth when I knew you were aware how my stepfather had unconsciously betrayed his friends? You judged us both as undesirables, therefore any attempt at explanation would, I know, only aggravate our offence in your eyes. Ah! You do not know how intensely I have suffered! How bitter it all was! I knew the reason you followed us to France - to watch and confirm your suspicions."

"I admit, Enid, that I suspected you of being in the hands of a set of scoundrels," her lover said in a low, hoarse voice. "At first I hesitated whether to warn you of your peril after Weirmarsh had, with such dastardly cunning, betrayed you to the French police, but - well," he added as he looked again into her dear eyes long and earnestly, "I loved you, Enid," he blurted forth. "I told you so! Remember, dear, what you said at Biarritz? And I love you - and because of that I resolved to save you!"

"Which you did," she said in a strained, mechanical tone. "We both have you to thank for our escape. Weirmarsh, having first implicated Paul, then made allegations against us, in order to send us to prison, because he feared lest my stepfather might, in a fit of remorse, act indiscreetly and make a confession."

"The past will all be forgiven now that Sir Hugh has been able to expose and unmask Weirmarsh and his band," Walter assured her. "A great sensation may possibly result, but it will, in any case, show that even though an Englishman may be bought, he can still remain honest.

203

And," he added, "it will also show them that there is at least one brave woman in England who sacrificed her love - for I know well, Enid, that you fully reciprocate the great affection I feel towards you - in order to bear her noble part in combating a wily and unscrupulous gang."

"It was surely my duty," replied the girl simply, her eyes downcast in modesty. "Yet association with that dastardly blackguard, Dr. Weirmarsh, was horrible! How I refrained from turning upon him through all those months I cannot really tell. I detested him from the first moment Sir Hugh invited him to our table; and though I went to assist him under guise of consultations, I acted with one object all along," she declared, her eyes raised to his and flashing, "to expose him in his true guise - that of Josef Blot, the head of the most dangerous association of forgers, of international thieves and blackmailers known to the police for the past half a century."

"Which you have surely done! You have revealed the whole plot, and confounded those who were so cleverly conspiring to effect a sudden and most gigantic coup. But —" and he paused, still looking into her eyes through his pince-nez, and sighed.

"But what?" she asked, in some surprise at his sudden change of manner.

"There is one matter, Enid, which" - and he paused - "well, which is still a mystery to me, and I - I want you to explain it," he said in slow deliberation.

"What is that?" she asked, looking at him quickly.

"The mystery which you have always refused to assist me in unravelling - the mystery of the death of Harry Bellairs," was his quiet reply. "You held him in high esteem; you loved him," he added in a voice scarce above a whisper.

She drew back, her countenance suddenly blanched as she put her hand quickly to her brow and reeled slightly as though she had been dealt a blow.

Walter watched her in blank wonderment.

CHAPTER XXXI

IN WHICH SIR HUGH TELLS HIS STORY

"You know the truth, don't you, dearest?" Walter asked at last in that quiet, sympathetic tone which he always adopted towards her whom he loved so well.

Enid nodded in the affirmative, her face hard and drawn.

"He was killed, was he not - deliberately murdered?"

For a few seconds the silence was unbroken save for a whir of a taxicab passing outside.

"Yes," was her somewhat reluctant response.

"You went to his rooms that afternoon," Walter asserted point blank.

"I do not deny that. I followed him home - to - to save him."

There was a break in her voice as she stammered out the last words, and tears rushed into her dark eyes.

"From what? From death?"

"No, from falling a prey to a great temptation set before him."

"By whom?"

"By the doctor, to whom my stepfather had introduced him," was the girl's reply. "I discovered by mere chance that the doctor, who had somewhat got him into his clutches, had approached him in order to induce him to allow him to take a wax impression of a certain safe key belonging to a friend of his named Thurston, a diamond broker in Hatton Garden. He had offered him a very substantial sum to do this - a sum which would have enabled him to clear off all his debts and start afresh. Harry's younger brother Bob had got into a mess, and in helping him out Harry had sadly entangled himself and was practically face to face with bankruptcy. I knew this, and I knew what a great temptation had been placed before him. Fearing lest, in a moment of despair, he might accept, I went, by appointment, to his chambers as soon as I arrived in London. Barker, his man, had been sent out, and we were alone. I found him in desperation, yet to my great delight he had defied Weirmarsh, saying he refused to betray his friend."

"And what did Bellairs tell you further?"

"He expressed suspicion that my stepfather was in the doctor's pay," she replied. "I tried to convince him to the contrary, but Weirmarsh's suggestion had evidently furnished the key to some suspicious document which he had one day found on Sir Hugh's writing-table."

"Well?"

"Well," she went on slowly, "we quarrelled. I was indignant that he should suspect my stepfather, and he was full of vengeance against Sir Hugh's friend the doctor. Presently I left, and – and I never saw him again alive!"

"What happened?"

"What happened is explained by this letter," she replied, crossing to a little buhl bureau which she unlocked, taking out a sealed envelope. On breaking it open and handing it to him she said: "This is the letter he wrote to me with his dying hand. I have kept it a secret – a secret even from Sir Hugh."

Walter read the uneven lines eagerly. They grew more shaky and more illegible towards the end, but they were sufficient to make the truth absolutely clear.

"Tonight, half an hour ago," (wrote the dying man) "I had a visit from your friend, Weirmarsh. We were alone, with none to overhear, so I told him plainly that I intended to expose him. At first he became defiant, but presently he grew apprehensive, and on taking his leave he made a foul accusation against you. Then, laughing at my refusal to accept his bribe, the scoundrel took my hand in farewell. He must have had a pin stuck in his glove, for I felt a slight scratch across the palm. At the moment I was too furious to pay any attention to it, but ten minutes after he had gone I began to experience a strange faintness. I feel now fainter . . . and fainter . . . A strange feeling has crept over me . . . I am dying . . . poisoned . . . by that king of thieves!

"Come to me quickly . . . at once . . . Enid . . . and tell me that what he has said against you . . . is not true. It . . . it cannot be true. . . . Don't delay. Come quickly. . . . Can't write more. - Harry."

Walter paused for a second after reading through that dramatic letter, the last effort of a dying man.

"And that scoundrel Weirmarsh killed him because he feared exposure," he remarked in a low, hard voice. "Why did you not bring this forward at the inquest?"

"For several reasons," replied the girl. "I feared the doctor's reprisals. Besides, he might easily have denied the allegation, or he might have used the same means to close my lips if he had suspected that I had learnt the truth."

"The dead man's story is no doubt true," declared Fetherston. "He used some deadly poison - one of the newly discovered ones which leaves no trace - to kill his victim who, in all probability, was not his first. Your stepfather does not know, of course, that this letter exists?"

"No. I have kept it from everyone. I said that the summons I received from him I had destroyed."

"In the circumstances I will ask you, Enid, to allow me to retain it," he said. "I want to show it to Trendall."

"You may show it to Mr. Trendall, but I ask you, for the present, to make no further use of it," replied the girl.

He moved a step closer to her and caught her disengaged hand in his, the glad light in her eyes telling him that his action was one which she reciprocated, yet some sense of her unworthiness of this great love causing her to hesitate.

"I will promise," said the strong, manly fellow in a low tone. "I ought to have made allowances, but, in the horror of my suspicion, I did not, and I'm sorry. I love you, Enid – I had never really loved until I met you, until I held your hand in mine!"

Enid's true, overburdened heart was only too ready to respond to his fervent appeal. She suffered her lover to draw her to himself, and their lips met in a long, passionate caress that blotted out all the past. He spoke quick, rapid words of ardent affection. To Enid, after all the hideous events she had passed through, it seemed too happy to be true that so much bliss was in store for her, and she remained there, with Walter's arm around her, silently content, that fervid kiss being the first he had ever imprinted upon her full red lips.

Thus they remained in each other's arms, their two true hearts beating in unison, their kisses mingling, their twin souls united in the first moments of their newly-found ecstasy of perfect love.

The fight had been a fierce one, but their true hearts had won, and, as they whispered each other's fond affection, Enid promised to be the wife of the honest, fearless man of whose magnificent work in the detection of crime the country had never dreamed. They read his books and were enthralled by them, but little did they think that he was one of the never-sleeping watch-dogs upon great criminals, or that the sweet-faced girl, who was now his affianced wife, had risked her life, her love, her honour, in order to assist him.

Next afternoon Sir Hugh called upon Walter at his dingy chambers in Holles Street, and as they sat together the old general, after a long and somewhat painful silence, exclaimed:

"I know, Fetherston, that you must be mystified how, in my position, I should have become implicated in the doings of that criminal gang."

"Yes, I am," Walter declared.

"Well, briefly, it occurred in this way," said the old officer. "While I was a colonel in India just before the war I was very hard pressed for money and had committed a fault – an indiscretion for which I might easily have been dismissed from the army. On being recalled to London, after war had been declared, I was approached by the fellow Weirmarsh who, to my horror, had, by some unaccountable means, obtained knowledge of my indiscretion! At first he adopted a high moral tone, upbraiding me for my fault and threatening to inform against me. This I begged him not to do. For a fortnight he kept me in an agony of despair, when one day he called me to him and unfolded to me a scheme by which I could make a considerable amount of money; indeed, he promised to pay me a yearly sum for my assistance."

"You thought him to be a doctor – and nothing else?" Walter said.

"Exactly. I never dreamed until quite recently that he was head of such a formidable gang, whose operations were upon so extensive a scale as to endanger our national credit," replied Sir Hugh. "At the time he approached me I was in the Pay Department, and many thousands of pounds in Treasury notes were passing through my safe weekly. His suggestion was that I should exchange the notes as they came to me from the Treasury for those with which he would supply me, and which, on showing me a specimen, I failed to distinguish from the real. I hesitated; I was hard up. To sustain my position after my knighthood money was absolutely necessary to me, and for a long time I had been unable to make both ends meet. The bait he dangled before me was sufficiently tempting, and – and – well, I fell!" he groaned, and then after a pause he went on:

"Whence Weirmarsh obtained the packets of notes which I substituted for genuine ones was, of course, a mystery, but once having taken the false step it was not my business to inquire. Not until quite recently did I discover his real position as chief of a gang of international crooks, who combined forgery with blackmail and theft upon a colossal scale. That he intended Bellairs should furnish him with an impression of the safe key of a diamond dealer in Hatton Garden is now plain. Bellairs defied him and threatened to denounce him to the police. Therefore, the poor fellow's lips were quickly closed by the scoundrel, who would hesitate at nothing in order to preserve his guilty secrets."

"But what caused you to break from him at last?" inquired Walter eagerly.

"Just before the armistice he and his friends had conceived a gigantic scheme by which Europe and the United States were to be flooded with great quantities of spurious paper currency, and though it would, when discovered – as it must have been sooner or later – have injured the national credit, would bring huge fortunes to him and his friends. He was pressing me to send in my papers and go to America, there to act as their agent at a huge remuneration. They wanted a man of standing who should be above suspicion, and he had decided to use me as his tool to engineer the gigantic frauds."

"And you, happily, refused?"

"Yes. I resolved, rather than act further, to relinquish the handsome payments he made to me from time to time. For that reason I got transferred from the Pay Department, so that I could no longer be of much use to him, a fact which annoyed him greatly."

"And he threatened you?"

"Yes. He was constantly doing so. He wanted me to go to New York. Enid helped me and gave me courage to defy him – which I did. Then he conceived a dastardly revenge by anonymously denouncing Le Pontois as a forger, and implicating both Enid and myself. He contrived that some money I brought from England should be exchanged for spurious notes, and these Paul unsuspiciously gave into the Crédit Lyonnais. Had it not been for your timely warning, Fetherston, we should both have also been arrested in France without a doubt."

"Yes," replied the other. "I was watching, and realised your peril, though I confess that my position was one of extreme difficulty. I, of course, did not know the actual truth, and, to be frank, I suspected both Enid and yourself of being implicated in some very serious crime."

"So we were," he said in a low, hard voice.

"True. But you have both been the means of revealing to the Treasury a state of things of which they never dreamed, and by turning King's evidence and giving the names and addresses of members of the gang in Brussels and Paris, all of whom are now under arrest, you have saved the country from considerable peril. Had the plot succeeded, a very serious state of things must have resulted, for the whole of our paper currency would have been suspected. For that reason the authorities have, I understand, now that they have arrested the gang and seized their presses, decided to hush up the whole matter."

"You know this?" asked Sir Hugh, suddenly brightening.

"Yes, Trendall told me so this morning."

"Ah! Thank Heaven!" he gasped, much relieved. "Then I can again face the world a free man. God knows how terribly I suffered through all those years of the war. I paid for my fault very dearly - I assure you, Fetherston."

CHAPTER XXXII

CONCLUSION

What remains to be related is quickly told, though the public have, until now, been in ignorance of the truth.

Out of evil a great good had come. At noon on the following day Trendall had an interview with Josef Blot, alias Weirmarsh, in his cell at Chelmsford, whither he had been conveyed by the police. What happened at that interview will never be known. It is safe to surmise, however, that the tragic letter of Harry Bellairs was shown to him – Enid having withdrawn her request that no use should be made of it. An hour after the chief of the Criminal Investigation Department had left, the prisoner was found lying stark dead, suffering from a scratch on the wrist, inflicted with a short, hollow needle which he had carried concealed behind the lapel of his coat.

Greatly to the discomfiture of the gang, the man Granier and his servant Pietro were extradited to France for trial, while a quantity of jewellery, works of art, money and negotiable securities of all sorts were unearthed from a villa near Fontainebleau and restored to their owners.

A fortnight after Weirmarsh's death, at St. George's, Hanover Square, Enid Orlebar became the wife of Walter Fetherston, and among the guests at the wedding were a number of strange men in whose position or profession nobody pretended to be interested. Truth to tell, they were officials of various grades from Scotland Yard, surely the most welcome among the wedding guests.

Though Walter and Enid live in idyllic happiness in a charming old ivy-grown manor house in Sussex, with level lawns and shady rose arbours, they still retain that old cottage at Idsworth, where a plausible excuse has been given to the country folk for "Mr. Maltwood" having been compelled to change his name. No pair in the whole of England are happier today.

No man holds his wife more dear, or has a more loving and hopeful companion. Their life is one of perfect and abiding peace and of sweet content.

Walter Fetherston is not by any means idle, for in his quiet country home he still writes those marvellous mystery stories which hold the world breathlessly enthralled, but he continues to devote half his time to combating the ingenuity of the greater criminals with all its attendant excitement and adventure, which are reflected in his popular romances.

Thank you for choosing this book – I hope you enjoyed it. Please be sure to visit oleanderpress.com to sign up for our infrequent, non-spammy Newsletter and get:

A free classic text
Updates on new LONDON BOUND titles
Complete list of all LONDON BOUND titles
Pre-order discounts
Special Offers
Exclusive Offers
As well as news of other Oleander titles.

For further benefits:
facebook.com/oleanderpress
Twitter.com/oleanderman

I'd also appreciate any comments – good and bad – on the current list and welcome ideas for new classic titles to publish – info@oleanderpress.com

I look forward to hearing from you!

Jon Gifford
Publisher,
Oleander Press